NECROPOLIS

NECROPOLIS

GUY PORTMAN

ONE

I T IS THE DAY of the church outing to the landmark
Beachy Head on the South Coast. My fourteen-year-old self
is straggling at the rear of the group when grinning cousin
Beatrice emerges beside me, and says, *Bet you wouldn't dare go
to the cliff edge. You're too scared to. And too gay like your dead
dad.* I march over to the edge of the cliff. Beatrice follows. *It*
slips on the grass and dangles from the precipice by its
fingertips. *Pull me up! Pull me up I said!* When I take the
penknife from my pocket, it stops pleading and starts wailing. I
bend down and saw off a braided pigtail. *NO!* With my foot I
swipe its fingers off the cliff edge. *Help!* I watch the shrieking,
chubby-cheeked face plummet into the grey mist.

'You're grinning, Dyson. Something funny?' The head of
housing here at the borough council where I work is approaching my desk. I return the braided, blonde pigtail that I am
holding to the drawer and close it. He stops adjacent to my
chair, leans into me, and whispers, 'Would suggest you wipe
that grin off your face before we get to the funeral.' He taps me
on the shoulder, then glances at his watch. 'Nearly time to go.'

'Yes, it is.'

He wanders off. The funeral is for the long-time former
head of my department – Burials and Cemeteries.

*

Twenty minutes later – I am ambling up the bitumen path that bisects Newton New Cemetery. This twenty-acre site is one of the burial grounds that I am responsible for. On either side of the path are graves. As I walk, I run my fingers along my black python-skin tie. The sombre and elegant garment is combined with a white dress shirt and dark grey suit, which is augmented with a pink handkerchief tucked into the jacket's breast pocket. I pass a gravesite brimming with pebble-sized, lilac marble-effect chips. On the gravesite's four corners are white ornamental cherubs slouched against hearts. These tacky, factory-produced mannequins share none of the realism and intricate detail of their Renaissance predecessors. I call them Essex Cherubs.

As I traverse the path, I consider what the forthcoming service will entail. There will be the ubiquitous garish bouquets, plywood casket, weeping relatives in cheap, ill-fitting outfits from bottom-end retail brands, and music consisting of modern electric organ and soppy songs, by artists such as George Michael and Celine Dion. After the ceremony refreshments will be served in the funeral hall – custard cream biscuits, lukewarm tea, and low-grade box wine.

The head of housing is chatting with people on the chapel's steps. His belly is protruding from his unbuttoned suit jacket. I go inside and take a seat in one of the middle rows. The crematorium and chapel caretaker is standing in a corner, blowing his nose on a less than pristine length of toilet paper. He acknowledges me with a nod. I reciprocate in kind. The hall is filling with people. They converge in small groups and chat, before dispersing amongst the rows of chairs. Sporadic sobs are audible. As I sit waiting for the commencement of the proceedings, I assure myself that my own funeral will have nothing in common with this.

In my mind's eye, I see a classically inspired mausoleum with Ionic columns. Along the white-pebbled path leading to the mausoleum are orderly rows of mourners. The sound of hooves announces the arrival of the hearse. It is hauled by twelve black Friesian horses. A troop of uniformed trumpeters play the first movement of Chopin's *Funeral March*. The harmonious scene is interrupted by the piercing screech of static emanating from the front of the hall, where the chaplain is struggling with a microphone. Following several more auditory violations, the crematorium and chapel caretaker bounds to the front and fiddles with the microphone. The chaplain says, 'We are here today to celebrate Dorothy's life.'

A motley group of coffin bearers shuffle along the central aisle with a veneered MDF casket. My assumptions about the service prove to be correct. The sole hymn is *Amazing Grace* by John Newton. After the subpar rendition of the influential melody, a girl of twelve or so reads what is purportedly a poem, entitled *Dear Nan*. It leaves me, not for the first time, feeling somewhat concerned about the declining standards of the nation's education system. The chaplain tells the congregation to spend a minute reflecting in silence on our time spent with Dorothy. Memories from my seven years working with her materialise in my mind. There are custard cream biscuits, Dorothy's favourites, and Quality Streets, of which there was usually an open box on her desk. Floral frocks, Ryman notepads, Bic pens, and the *Daily Mail* open at the horoscopes page.

The service concludes with *My Heart Will Go On* by Celine Dion. I hastily weave through the departing congregation. Everyone makes their way to the burial plot. Two burly funeral workers lower the MDF casket into the hole. As I watch them, I fiddle with the braided pigtail in my trouser pocket. Three wreaths are deposited on the casket. There is the ubiquitous purple and lilac-mixed sheaf, a tacky pink and white-based posy wreath, and a personalised wreath with a trite message that reads *Sweet Dreams*. Everyone disperses in the direction of the funeral hall that adjoins the chapel. They do so with considerable fanfare, some sobbing, others shamelessly weeping. Inside the hall, I am approached by council employee and head of housing's cousin, Darren. He is employed in the council's refuse department.

'Alright?'

'Good afternoon.'

Darren's appearance is his customary carefully cultivated scruffiness. Shirt untucked, hair ruffled.

'Heavy one last night in Sarf London. Eight pints 'n some bangin' nose bag … Pulled this bird with a massive rack.'

'Congratulations.'

The repast consists of custard creams, pink wafers, lukewarm tea served in disposable cups, cheap box wine, and cans of Stella Artois. Darren picks up a can and says, 'Fancy a wife beater?'

'Yes.'

It is preferable to the alternatives.

*

That evening – I am in my living room, reading Antony Beevor's narrative history *Stalingrad*, when the doorbell sounds. I put the book down, go over to the front door and peer through the peephole. My girlfriend Eva is wearing tight-fitting jeans and a tank top. She lives in the adjoining block to here. On opening the door, she shrieks, 'Dyson!' and throws her arms around my neck. Having taken a step back she examines my suited self. 'You look really smart even by your standards. Where have you been?'

'A funeral.'

She waves her hand and says, 'Don't tell me any more.' I close the door. 'Do you mind if I watch a bit of TV?'

'Go ahead.'

Until recently Eva had a television of her own. She claims it broke, but I am convinced she sold it to buy drugs. In the living room, Eva picks the controller up off the coffee table, switches on the television, and flicks through the channels until she reaches the singing talent show, *X Factor*. I say, 'Oh no.'

'Don't be like that.'

The contestant is a plump woman in dire need of a dentist. She has a Midlands accent; her name begins with S. Her choice of song is *My Heart Will Go On* by Celine Dion. I clench my teeth to prevent myself bellowing an obscenity. Eva says, 'Is everything okay?' I stand up. 'Where are you going?'

'Leaving.'

Eva crosses her arms, and says, 'Fine.'

As I go through to the kitchen, I consider that there is an uncanny resemblance between wannabe warbler S's teeth and a pre-makeover Celine Dion. Particularly the unnaturally long, sharp incisors; the reason for a Quebec-based magazine having given the young Celine Dion the nickname *Canine Dion*. After dragging a chair over to the far wall, I switch on the fan above the oven to drown out Dion's wails. I resume reading.

The Soviet T-34 tank was arguably the most significant invention of the twentieth century. If it were not for the T-34, Hitler may very well have crushed the Soviet Union and won The War.

'Why is the fan on?' Eva is standing in the kitchen's entrance. '*X Factor* is over and there's a programme on you might like.'

The programme is about war criminals who have not yet been captured and brought to justice. There is a Hutu general with genocidal tendencies, a tyrannical Congolese warlord, and a Liberian commander with a penchant for blood diamonds. The next to be featured is a Serbian militia leader, who allegedly committed atrocities against Croats during the Yugoslav Wars.

Eva is cowering in the corner of the sofa sucking her thumb. She hails from Croatia. She emigrated here with her parents shortly after hostilities commenced. The alleged war criminal is Darko Draganović, a member of the much-maligned Serb Volunteer Guard. There is footage of him rolling around on a floor with a tiger cub, posing with his comrades in the stands at a Red Star Belgrade game, and guzzling beer in a strip bar. This large, jovial-looking man is strangely familiar. I have come across him somewhere before. There have been purported sightings of Darko Draganović in Belgium and the UK.

TWO

THE CHANGING ROOM DOOR bursts open and school children pour in. At the front of the group is fellow pupil, cousin, and piece of detritus, Beatrice. Its pigtails are dangling menacingly from the sides of its head. *Bog flush him* it screams. The children pick me up by the arms and legs and carry me off, to the accompaniment of Beatrice's high-pitched, exuberant shrieks. I am hoisted into the toilets and held by my ankles above a toilet bowl. In the murky water, a coiled turd is visible. I try to wriggle free from their grasp. Headfirst I am lowered into the bowl.

I awaken with my heartbeat reverberating in my chest. It is nearly six o'clock. For the next twenty minutes I lie in bed, thinking about nemesis Beatrice, the daughter of my mother's sister. It was in the class two years above me at school. I had to put up with daily bullying from it and its classmates. If only I could kill it again. I punch my pillow. After washing and getting dressed for work, I take from my chest of drawers the fly-fishing tin Mother bought me for my seventh birthday. I open it and brush my fingertips over the contents – braided pigtail, crucifix necklace, earring, and monocle. I remove the pigtail, hold it up and relive the event when this memento came into my possession. It is nearly time to leave for work. I return the pigtail to the fly-fishing tin, pick up the crucifix necklace, and exit the flat.

Having dropped my empty cup of caffè latte extra hot with soya milk in a bin, I enter the office. What with it being early, the open-plan workspace is near empty. On my left is the housing department, and on my right social services. Up ahead I can see HR's Emma. She spins her revolving office chair towards me.

'Hi Dyson.'

'Good morning.'

'How are you?'

'Fine.'

In Burials and Cemeteries, I sit down at my desk and switch on the computer. As I wait for it to start, I fiddle with the crucifix necklace, reminiscing as I do so on how it came into my possession. It used to belong to Virulent Veronica, who along with her sister, Conniving Clementine, owned the café in the town where I lived as a child.

'Morning, Dyson.'

It is my assistant Asma. She was off yesterday. I say, 'Good morning.'

'How did the funeral go?'

'As expected.' She sits down at the desk opposite me and logs into her computer. 'Today, you will be continuing with updating the spreadsheet for the online death register.'

'Yes. Will get on it as soon as I've dealt with the inbox.'

Asma is having an arranged marriage in Yemen. She will not be returning to Burials and Cemeteries. This is annoying, as the chances of finding such an able replacement are remote.

An hour later – I am clasping my National Association of Funeral Directors mug and a green teabag. On the approach to Emma's desk, I increase my pace to avoid a potential interaction. In the kitchen I switch on the kettle. While I wait for it to boil, I finger the crucifix necklace. My eleven-year-old self was walking along the high street in town when Virulent Veronica emerged from her café. She prodded me with a pole and screamed at me to stay away from her and her customers, lest I contract them with the evil AIDS virus that had recently killed my father. It was not to be the last of the abuse I would suffer at the hands of her and her vile sibling.

The kettle is boiled. Having poured the water, I press the teabag against the side of the mug with a teaspoon, until the water is a suitable shade of green. There is a copy of *The Sun* on the table. I flick through the piss rag. Terrence trudges in. Last year he had a failed hair transplant in Turkey. Darren is adamant that he has seen him trying to repair the damage with Pritt Stick. Today, as always, Terrence's hair is in a deplorable state. The long, lank strands on the sides of his head have been brushed upwards and gelled to the scalp, while the meagre remaining strands from the front have been clumped together at their bases and fanned out at the top.

'What's so funny?'

'Ha, something I'm reading.'

I leave. At the age of eighteen I returned to my childhood town. I found Virulent Veronica hanging clothes on a washing line in her garden. She was dispatched with an axe and the crucifix necklace plucked from her severed neck. Cancer got her sister, Conniving Clementine. If it hadn't, I would have. The telephone on my desk is ringing.

'Good morning, Burials and Cemeteries.'

'Is that Dyson Devereu-x?'

'Dyson Devereux. The X is silent.'

'Foreign name, must be.'

'Norman.'

'Dyson you said it was.'

This is the typical level of intellect I endure day in, day out, here at the council. The imbecile informs me that her husband is soon to die. She wants his ashes to be interred at Newton Old. I explain that only Newton New has availability. She protests vehemently and insists that he only likes Newton Old.

9

I tell her that there is no correlation between like and availability. By the end of the call, I am hoping that she will decide to join her husband and leap into the flaming cremator, Hindu-style.

A melee of female council workers are engaging in an animated discussion around the photocopier. I hear *X Factor* mentioned several times. A continual stream of council workers pass along the passageway close to my desk. Most pass by without comment. A few grunt 'Good morning', or something to that effect. The head of housing, Frank, says to me, 'Be in the foyer at one. We're going to the eight-pound fifty Chinese buffet.'

*

13:49 – The Mandarin Tasty House – Darren prods at a grotesque, bread-crumbed crab claw impaled on Frank's fork, and says, 'What the fuck is that?'

'A crab claw,' replies Frank. 'Want one?'

'Nah.'

I say, 'Not even in the most polluted bowels of the Yangtze Delta would you find a crab claw looking like that.'

'They're not real,' says Frank. 'Well, the claw is. Bread-crumbed part has been stuffed with other meats.'

Darren says, 'Rank.'

I say, 'Any leftovers or reconstituted meat could be hidden beneath those breadcrumbs.'

'Guess so,' says Frank. He nibbles on his crab claw. 'Darren.'

'What?'

'You should have come to the fish place with me and Dyson, err, week before last. By the canal it is.' Frank has a gulp of beer. 'Remember, Dyson, the last time you graced me with your presence at lunch?'

'Yes, I remember Armenian Fish Bar.'

'It's not called that,' says Frank.

'What's the grub like?' says Darren.

'Had a burger,' says Frank. 'Was edible, just. Dyson here ordered something called a, err, fish dinero.'

'What the fuck is that?'

I say, 'The picture on the menu gave the impression it was fish and chips.'

Frank swallows a mouthful of noodles, and says, 'Didn't turn out that way, did it?'

'Indeed not. It was an Armenian-inspired infusion of cheap sardinella and bottom-feeding cusks.'

Frank and Darren laugh. Frank chokes on his noodles. His face reddens. He gulps from his bottle of Tsing Tao beer and wipes tears from his cheeks with a tissue.

'Where's Arm-enia?' says Darren. He looks at Frank, then at me. 'Africa?'

I say, 'No wonder you ended up working in bins.'

Darren flicks a middle finger at me. Frank says, 'Be nice, Dyson. Armenia used to be part of the USSR, didn't it?'

'Yes. It is bordered by Turkey, Georgia, Azerbaijan and Iran.'

'What's it famous for?' says Darren. 'Other than crap cafs?'

I say, 'KGB interrogators.'

'The Kardashians came from there, originally.'

Who are the Kardashians?

'Never heard of 'em,' says Darren.

Frank sighs and his shoulders slump. He says, 'The Kardashians have a reality TV show.' I groan. 'Daughter and wife watch it. Started last year, I think.' He clicks his fingers. 'Yeah, last year, 2007. Got a horrible feeling we're going to be stuck with the Kardashians for years to come.' He wipes his face with a napkin. 'Much as I'd love to sit here all day, best be getting back to the coalface. I'll get this.' He pulls out a wallet. I am fiddling with the crucifix necklace in my trouser pocket when he says, 'By the way, Dyson, drove past one of your cemeteries

11

this morning. Newton Old it was. Saw your maintenance team working there. The new one, big hulking chap he is. Has a face on him like a child's funeral.'

*

The following morning – I am clearing Dead Dorothy's desk. Having fed a *Daily Mail* horoscope page into the shredder, I pick a card off her desk. It has a hand-drawn picture of a rainbow on it, and a grinning face with the words *I Love Nan* scrawled beneath it. I shove the card in the shredder. Wedged in the gap between the desk and the window are two more cards. The first is of the get well soon variety and has a picture of a teddy bear reposing in a hospital bed. People do not get well soon after being diagnosed with terminal cancer. They don't get well ever, so why do people insist on sending cards of this ilk, when a condolence card would be more appropriate?

The second card has a picture of a cross and a dove with a leaf in its beak, below which is a new age hymn titled *Rejoice in Zion*. The sport, leisure and culture department manager sent it. The card is thicker than the others and the shredder struggles. I give it a push to hasten the process. Frank is approaching. I nudge the shredder under my desk with my foot, so that he does not see what is being shredded. I possess highly evolved social intuition and am aware that he won't appreciate seeing it.

Frank says, 'Will take a while to get used to coming over here and not being offered a Quality Street. Dorothy would always save a triangle or swirl for me, no matter what.' He sighs. 'Taken before her time.' His mobile phone is ringing. He answers it. 'On my way.' He hangs up. 'Family's going to the in-laws Saturday afternoon, and I'm a free man. Fancy a round of golf at Ruislip?'

'What time?'

'Two o'clock.'

'Sure, count me in.'

'Look forward to it.'

Frank trots off in the direction of housing. Soon after I go to my work appraisal. Sunita is one of the council's most senior employees. She is presently rummaging through a filing cabinet. A hefty, wiggling posterior wrapped in a pink skirt is aimed at me, reminding me of a pig at a trough. I turn away from the offending sight and look through the internal office's glass wall. The scene here on floor eight is no different from my floor, floor seven. Chattering people are gathered around a photocopier machine. Others are hunched over keyboards. On their desks are piles of paper and desk tidies, from which sprout Bic pens and scissors.

Sunita is sitting behind her desk scouring a file with small, brown beady eyes. In the middle of her forehead there is a *bindi* dot. The face is dominated by a garish red lipstick smear that serves as a mouth. The red smear moves.

'Your work has been satisfactory ... We've received no serious complaints of late.' *This is going well.* But then she says, 'We have decided to increase your annual salary by two and a half thousand.'

No way, she can't be serious. I say, 'Is this a joke?'

She isn't smiling like most people do when they tell jokes, and at any rate Sunita doesn't tell jokes. She looks at me, and says, 'No, this is not a joke.'

'I know that Dorothy earned six thousand more than what you are proposing.'

'Think of this as a trial run.'

'A trial marathon! I've been running the department since she went into hospital.'

Sunita attempts to placate me with marginally improved pension benefits. I will the blood-red *bindi* in the middle of its forehead to tremor. This to be followed by a pop as the back of

13

Sunita's head explodes. I picture red mist spraying on the glass wall behind it and it slumping to the floor. But the *bindi* remains unscathed. That *bindi* is nothing more than a fashion statement-cum-ingratiating, politically correct gesture. Sunita is not even a genuine Hindu, I have seen it eating Big Macs in the mall. It drones on about what the council describes as *the bigger picture*, plans for the future, and how lucky I am to be a part of *this exciting project*. The telephone on its desk is ringing. It picks it up, and says into it, 'Will be down in one second.' Having placed a henna-stained appendage over the receiver, it says, 'Come back in ten minutes with a cappuccino for me.'

Ill-mannered ingrate. I get up and leave. Perhaps I'll add a dribble of urine, drops of semen, or the contents of a nostril to that cappuccino.

*

The next day – Asma announces, 'Here are the laminates.'

I take them, survey them, and say, 'You've increased the font size. Our visually impaired cemetery visitors will be satisfied.'

'Ah, yes they will.' She takes a brown-padded envelope off her desk and passes it to me. 'This came from DHL.'

I open it and empty the contents on my desk. Tightly bound with elastic bands are the new identity cards for my cemetery staff. I unwrap the bands and count the cards. Will get over to Boden right away and distribute them.

*

Boden, at a little over five acres, is the second largest of my three cemeteries. It was built in the 1700s, though most of the graves are nineteenth and early twentieth century. This burial ground is a sombre enclave, devoid of Essex cherubs. It is

14

enclosed on all sides by towering chestnut trees and inter-spersed with traditional grey tombstones. There is a small memorial garden at one end and a Crimean War memorial obelisk at the other. I stroll up the narrow path that bisects the facility, either side of which are piles of raked leaves. There are numerous motley-colored pigeons pecking at the ground. Their presence is due to the crazy woman who feeds them. I will be contacting the council's pest control unit.

Three men holding rakes are stationed near the memorial obelisk. They are wearing green coats with Newton Borough Council printed on their backs. Tucked into the waistbands of their trousers are black plastic refuse bags. One of the men, a former amphetamine addict from Glasgow named Angus, is scampering down the path. He is clasping his rake as if it were a spear. He calls out, 'Alright, Big Man?'

'Not bad. And yourself?'

'Cannae complain.'

He stands in front of me with his mouth open, revealing his few remaining teeth, which have been worn down by years of amphetamine-fueled grinding.

'Where is Rebecca?'

'Rebecca?'

'Yes, Rebecca.'

'Dinnae know.' Rebecca is the caretaker of Boden. She is supposed to be here supervising the leaf clearing. Angus shouts, 'Cheikhee!'

Cheikh comes over. Angus proceeds to rake the few remain-ing leaves left on the path at a frenetic pace. Having removed a glove, Cheikh shakes my hand vigorously.

'*Bonjour Cheikh, ca va?*'

'*Ca va bien, Monsieur Devereux.*'

'*Ou'est Rebecca?*'

'Park, ah, Newton Green.'

That would make sense, as Rebecca also oversees Newton

Green and its adventure playground. I pass him his new identification card, he thanks me. Angus takes his, holds it up at eye level, and says, 'Bonnie card.'

'Indeed.' I am examining the new addition to the team's card when he lumbers over. Frank is not wrong, Kiro Burgan does indeed have a face like a child's funeral. He is well over six-foot, has a burly physique, thick, greying hair, and green eyes. 'Good afternoon.'

After grunting 'Hello', he grabs his ID card off me with a large paw. I am looking at him. 'What?'

'There is a ten-pound fee to replace lost cards. So I suggest you lot take good care of them. Good day.'

The hulking, humorless temp was supplied by an employment agency last month. I have only seen him on a couple of occasions. It is already four o'clock and there is no point in returning to the office. I will finish my remaining work from home. The journey is made on the number seventy-seven bus. Back at my flat, I send four emails and do some computations for my department's financial forecast spreadsheets.

It is early evening, and I am in the living room reading Stalingrad. The doorbell sounds. I go over to the door and peer through the peephole. It is Eva. I open the door.

'Good evening.'

'Hi.' Eva steps into the flat. I close the door. 'Been thinking we should do something this evening. It's Friday after all, let's go out for a change. The pub on the high street has just reopened.'

'Yes, I saw.'

'My friend says it's really good. She went there the other day and …'

Kiro Burgan reminds me of the Serbian militia leader from the programme about war criminals that was on after *X Factor*. The notable difference between the men is that Kiro Burgan is sour-faced and grumpy, while the alleged Serbian war criminal appeared jovial. If he is the same person, which is highly improbable, this difference could be explained by the fact that he has swapped tiger cub, football match, strip club and beer for a rake and bin bags.

THREE

THE FOLLOWING MONDAY – Newton Community and Business Facility is hosting the quarterly cemeteries and funeral business professionals meeting. Most of the people employed in the death industry in Newton Borough and the adjoining boroughs are in attendance, both public and private sector employees. On my left a Lithuanian gravedigger is picking his nose. On my right a mortician is playing a game on his mobile phone. Next to him a bereavement counsellor's afro-styled head is lolling to one side. In the row in front a morgue rat is snoring. A fellow morgue rat in the adjoining seat glances at her watch and utters an obscenity in an Eastern European language. The heavyset figure a few rows ahead with spiky hair is Rebecca, the overseer of Boden.

At the front of the hall, a local female Conservative councillor is giving a presentation about teamwork. It is the same tripe I have heard infinite times. Seeing Rebecca reminds me of Kiro Burgan. When I return to the office, I will reacquaint myself with that programme about war criminals. There is a high probability it is on *YouTube*. Of course, the chances of it being him are akin to winning a meaningful prize on the lottery. A wanted, alleged war criminal wouldn't likely be hiding in plain sight, unless they had undergone a complete makeover, not merely changing their expression.

The councilor disembarks the stage, signaling the start of the mid-morning break. Teamwork is of scant concern as a rush of death business personnel descend on the table at the rear of the hall, where plates of custard creams, pink wafers, orange squash, and tea served in disposable cups awaits. I squeeze between two turbaned figures then push past a plump bereavement counsellor, who squeals, 'Excuse me!'

Having deposited three pink wafers on a plate, I leave the melee. Fraser Raven is heading my way. Fraser has the public funeral contract with the council. Public funerals are for those too poor to fund their own. After spitting a mouthful of what appears to be a custard cream into his Styrofoam cup, he says, 'Dry as a week-old cadaver. Give me a wafer!' He discards the cup on the windowsill then snatches one of my two remaining pink wafers. Fraser tells me how drunk he got last night. An all-day session in the pub was followed by a strip club. 'Got home at one to find that the wife had locked me out. Couldn't believe it. Well, I could.' Fraser wipes a greasy, black strand of hair off his forehead. 'Bitch!'

'You managed to get in then?'

'Did I fuck. Went to a mini-cab firm to get a ride to my office. They refused to take me; said I was too drunk. Ended up getting the night bus. Fell asleep, went two stops too far, and had to walk all the way back. Passed out on the slab in the mortuary. Woke up sick as a dog first thing. Surprised I didn't die of hypothermia in there. Freezing this time of year.'

'Well, the mortuary is for corpses, not the living.'

Rebecca strides over, and says, 'Morning, Dyson. Fraser, you look like shit.'

'Case of the pot calling the kettle black.'

She makes a huffing noise. I say, 'Rebecca, I have your new identification card.' Rebecca takes it and marches off. 'It's ten pounds for a replacement,' I call after her.

'Suck my dick, Dyson.'

'Charming,' says Fraser.

It is standard procedure for Rebecca. Good thing she is conscientious and works hard for me, otherwise I wouldn't put up with that sort of language.

*

The war criminals programme is not on *YouTube*. However, I am able to find the alleged Serbian war criminal, Darko Draganović, on *Google*. There are several photographs of Darko and some half-decent video footage of him prancing around in military fatigues with a tiger, a full-grown specimen this time. Having pressed pause, I minimise *YouTube* and study the digital proof of Kiro Burgan's identification card. There is a striking similarity between the two men. Sure, Kiro is approximately fifteen years older, marginally slimmer around the middle, greyer, and grumpier. After expanding the identification card proof, I examine Kiro's green eyes. They are the same colour as the war criminal's eyes, which can be clearly seen in one of the photographs.

Asma pads over to my desk with a brochure, I minimise the proof. She says, 'This is a brochure for Eco Eternal Rest Ltd. It came in this morning's post.' She puts it on my desk. I open it. 'What do you think?'

Environmentally friendly concepts have permeated everything in recent years, even death, as these durable, recycled plastic memory benches testify. The benches come in five colours, are durable, weatherproof, and have plaques, suitable for inscriptions of approximately twenty words.

'I will never allow these crudely fashioned eyesores to defile my cemeteries.'

'Oh!' she says. 'You really don't like them.'

'They are horrendous. Recycled plastic has no place in a cemetery.'

Asma tilts her head from side-to-side. Green eyes are relatively rare, present in approximately two percent of the population, and the majority of these are female. I know this because I, too, have green eyes. Darko/Kiro's eyes are very similar to my own. Ascetically pleasing, lucid, and intelligent. Fortunately for me and unfortunately for them/potentially him that is where the similarities between us end.

Having dumped the Eco Eternal Rest Ltd brochure in the bin, I go to the kitchen to make a green tea. On the way, HR's Emma swivels around in her revolving office chair, points at a framed photograph on her desk, and says, 'My five-year-old son, Casper. Isn't it just the cutest photo?' I view with disdain the perpetuation of her genetic repugnance's. 'We took Casper to a play centre this weekend. It was so much fun, watching him scamper about with the other kids. Did you do anything special on the weekend?'

Friday evening, I had a few drinks. On Saturday I played golf, and on Sunday I went to a gastro pub for lunch with Eva. I had a chicken and mushroom pie, which was probably the highlight of the weekend.

'I had a chicken and mushroom pie in a gastro pub. The *pâte feuilletée* was exquisite.'

'Pate feu-ill-etee?'

'*Pâte feuilletée* is French for puff pastry.'

*

07:15 – The following morning – Today, I am going with this silk, lilac tie from Forzieri. Having dabbed *eau de cologne* on my cheeks, I smooth down my brown hair with hair gel. In my full-length mirror, perfection is staring at me. The first appointment of the day is with Fraser at his funeral parlour. Revisions will be discussed regarding his public funeral contract with my department. Prior to that I am having breakfast at Starbucks with Eva … *Beeep*. That is my recently purchased Nokia mobile phone with a text message stating that she will meet me outside. I leave.

Eva is on the pavement smoking hash. When she sees me, she stubs the butt out on a lamppost and then flicks it away. Her face is pale and drawn. I say, 'Good morning.'

'Hi.'

'Had a big night?'

'Yes, was with friends. We had a, um, sort of party.' A flicker of a smile. 'Didn't get much sleep.'

Her appearance suggests she didn't get any. There is bruising around her eyes. She clutches my arm with a trembling hand. We go to Starbucks. After breakfast, I will do some research into the potential Kiro-Darko situation at an internet café. My internet was extremely slow last night, and it was barely functioning this morning.

In Starbucks, Eva leans against the glass front of a food display unit and gapes at the menu board. I will have a 'Caffè latte extra hot with soya milk and a *croque monsieur* panini, please … Eva. *Eva!*'

'What?'

'What are you having?'

'Um, one sec.' *She's been staring at the menu for ages.* 'Tuna melt and a skinny latte with soya milk.'

I am sipping coffee; Eva is fidgeting. She picks up her mug. Several drops spill on the table. I urge my panini to cool, as it is still too hot to eat. Eva starts talking about *our future together*. She uses the word *us* liberally. She says, 'We could start afresh somewhere. What do you think?'

'It's a possibility, I suppose.'

Eva clasps my fingers in hers. I pull my hand away and have a nibble on my panini. It is a good temperature. Breakfast is dragging on. It is high time I got over to the internet café. I have a bite of panini, then polish off my caffè latte. Eva says,

'Halloween is soon. I might go to this club with my friends for it. But it's fancy dress and I don't have a Halloween costume.'

'You could always go as yourself.'

Eva sits up straight in her seat, and says, 'What's that supposed to mean?'

'As the living dead is what I mean.' I point at the mirrored wall adjacent to us. 'Look.' Eva swivels in the direction of the mirror and immediately begins to sob. I push a paper serviette across the table. The sobbing escalates into crying. A woman in a trouser suit is looking this way, as is a man holding what looks to be a Caramel Frappuccino. I say, 'Stop crying!' but the crying increases in volume. I get up and leave. Eva chases after me. On the pavement, I say to her, 'It's apparent that your drug use is no longer recreational. This is an issue. I strongly suggest you give this matter serious consideration. Good day.'

I walk off. The internet café is remarkably busy for such an early hour. There is an available computer sandwiched between a computer occupied by a burka-clad figure, and one being used by a man in a shiny Eastern European-style shell suit.

I find a webpage that mentions the purported sightings of Darko Draganović in Belgium and the United Kingdom. There are no specific details about the sightings. Logic suggests, if not demands, that Darko would want to get further away from the International Court of Justice in The Hague, rather than closer to it. The webpage states that Darko has a large and distinctive tattoo on the underside of his left forearm – the Serbian crest, which consists of two eagles facing opposite ways beneath a crown. There is a link near the bottom of the page which I click on. It takes me to a webpage for a Croatian vigilante organisation. Halfway down it is a photograph of Darko, and beneath that is printed – *Reward for information leading to the capture of Darko Draganović – 1.5 million Euros.*

That is a handsome reward. Darko's purported ethnic cleansing methods evidently didn't endear him to this lot. It would take nearly two and a half decades to earn that sum in Burials and Cemeteries. Still, the chances of Kiro Burgan being Darko Draganović are remote.

*

I ring on Raven & Co. Funeral Directors' doorbell. Fraser's secretary opens the door.

'Morning, Dyson.'

'Good morning.'

'You look good as always.'

'You too.' And I mean it. She is petite, demure and blonde. Her hair was long on the last occasion I saw her but is now worn in a bob. 'You've changed your hair.'

'Yes.' She tilts her head to the side. 'You think it looks good?'

'I don't think; I know.'

'*Hi*, I like that.' She strokes my shoulder with long, red-varnished fingernails. 'Fraser's in the mortuary.'

Having slipped into the mortuary, I survey my surroundings. There are shelves brimming with jars, bottles and boxes. There is a six-corpse capacity mortuary fridge, an embalming machine, and several mortuary trays. The room's centrepiece, its altar, is a steel mortuary slab that rises graciously from the floor. Fraser is bent over it holding a makeup pencil. On the slab lies a corpse. Only its exposed feet and ankles are visible from where I am.

This silent enclave is an infinitely superior working environment to the council, which is grossly unfair. Fraser had the fortune of hailing from a dynasty of prestigious funeral directors, while I had a gay father who died of AIDS and a mother who perished from a prescription pill addiction when I was twelve. If only I'd been born with a jar of embalming fluid in my hand. If I had, I would never have ventured within a stone's throw of a local council.

'Jesus!' Fraser spins around. 'How long have you been in here for?'

'A few seconds.'

'Well, don't just stand there. Come on over.'

On the slab is a naked man in a state of repose. His eyes are half open, the pupils unfocused beneath their bleary veneer. Below the torso's grey-textured translucent surface, are green and purple blotches and dark veins. Rigid rolls of colourless skin form waves across the concave stomach. There are flattened, hardened folds of skin hanging from the torso's sides. They resemble defunct wings. The stomach is in stark contrast with the flabby shapeless limbs, laced with webs of varicose veins. It is as if the stomach went on a diet and forgot to tell the limbs. With dexterous swishes of the makeup pencil, Fraser blushes a cheek.

'Bloater here was found in the bath. Had been in there for days.' He wipes a strand of hair off his forehead with his sleeve. 'The block's caretaker let me in. Scarpered the instant he got a sniff of what was lurking inside … Only the balding head was visible above the browned waters.'

'Browned?'

'There was a film four, five centimetres thick of his own degradation.' Fraser prods with the makeup brush at a white-board on the wall. Two photographs are pinned to it. 'Photo on the left is Bloater on arrival.'

Bloater is indeed a befitting term for the specimen in this photograph. The ballooned carcass's grossly engorged body and limbs are covered in blue veins and discolouration. It has a swollen head, bulging eyes, and a purple tongue that lolls from the corner of its mouth. Bloater bears little resemblance to the cadaver on the slab. The second photograph is of a smartly dressed, smirking, chubby-cheeked child, around seven or so.

'Who is the kid?'

'That is Bloater at his First Communion. His mummy gave

25

me strict instructions that is how her little darling is to look on his big day, which is today, in …' Fraser checks his watch. 'Just over three hours.' He jabs with the makeup brush. 'His clothes are on that hanger over there.'

The clothes are a big version of what Bloater wore at his First Communion. School shorts, braces, white shirt, blue tie. On the floor are a polished pair of black shoes with shining buckles.

'Interesting choice of attire.'

'Not that out of the ordinary really. What Bloater's mummy requires for the wake is a candy-coated memory to remember her boy by. She wants to remember him as a sweet kid, not the grotesque, flatulent porker Bloater became.' Fraser is holding up a plastic container. 'Anti-fungal powder. I used it for the folds of fat. The last thing, well nearly, that you want at a funeral is fungal fat. Never good for repeat business.'

'Was he difficult to embalm?'

'Nightmare from the start.' Fraser shoves his hands in the pockets of his apron. 'First problem was the incision point. Normally, I opt for the femoral. It's on the inside of the thigh.'

'I know what a femoral is!'

'Okay.' Fraser touches the corpse's throat. 'With fatties and in bloating instances, the incision should be made at the carotid.'

'What is your rationale for that?'

'Anything with a BMI approaching Bloater here, you've got yellow butterfat, and lots of it. The femoral will be slippery as hell. Sure way to have butterfat spraying all over the place. Fat is extremely hazardous. Only last year in Germany a cremato-rium burnt down in a grease fire, all because the incinerating Kraut had gone a little crazy with the schnitzels, *ja*.'

'I see.' Bloater's cheeks are much slimmer than in the pho-tograph of him on arrival. 'How did you make them thinner?'

'Aha.' He taps his nose. 'Have a little trick up my sleeve for giving fatties that chiselled, male Armani underwear model look. Remove the fat from the inside of the cheek with a scalpel, and then stick the inside of the cheek to the teeth with adhesive. You ever seen *Zoolander*?'

'Yes, with Ben Stiller as the male model.' Fraser extends his arm towards the corpse. 'Behold, Magnum!'

'And how come the stomach looks so slim compared to the limbs? I take it you discarded some of the innards.'

'Ever observant, Dyson. Stomach, bladder and intestines are in the fridge.' His secretary totters into the mortuary with a tray containing a pot of tea and two cups. 'Perfect timing Sally, thank you.'

She pours the tea, winks at me, and leaves the mortuary. As we drink tea, Fraser drones on about the 'ongoing issues' with his wife. One and a half million Euros is an exorbitant amount for such an obscure alleged war criminal. That vigilante organisation must have some wealthy backers. I will discover more about the mysterious Kiro Burgan. Where does he claim to come from? What languages does he speak? And above all, does he have that distinctive tattoo?

'Dyson … Dyson!'

'Yes.'

'You were a million miles away.'

*

That afternoon – The calm ambience of the mortuary is but a distant memory. I am at my desk scrutinising a budget forecast spreadsheet while trying to ignore the council workers chattering all around me. Asma is on the telephone. It is apparent that she is talking to Pigeon Lady. Asma puts the telephone down, and says, 'Have the woman who feeds the pigeons on the line. She wants to speak to you.'

'Put her through.'

Presumably, pest control must have acted promptly for once on my demand to rid my cemetery of the varmint. I pick up the ringing telephone.

'DYSON! Is that you?'

'Yes.'

'The pigeons have disappeared. There are none in Boden. Not even one.'

'To be expected, madam. Pigeons are nomadic during late autumn. It is an evolutionary trait they are yet to correct.'

'Never heard that. Been pigeons all year round here in the past, and other places I feed them at. They'd come if ...'

I rip a piece of A4 from my pad, crumple it next to the receiver, and say, 'Your reception is bad, you're cutting out.'

I hang up. Asma covers her mouth with her palm. There is an envelope icon flashing on my computer screen. It is an email from Rebecca regarding subsiding graves at Boden; the ongoing problem having been exacerbated by the recent torrential rain. It would be but a simple task to instruct her by email of the actions I plan to employ. However, I will use this as a pretext to fix an appointment to visit her and pry for any information that she might have on Kiro Burgan. I telephone her.

'Yeah.'

'I have read your email.'

'And?'

'We should meet in person to discuss the affected graves.'

I hear her sigh. Seconds after terminating the conversation, my office telephone rings again. What now? I answer with, 'Good afternoon.'

'Sunita here. Come up to my office.'

Two minutes later – The *bindi* dot is untarnished and there is no red mist sprayed on the glass wall behind it. This is not a good start. I pull out a chair and sit on it. The corners of the garish red smear curl upwards. That's not good either.

'Good news, we've found a replacement for Asma.' *Better*

not be my previous assistant Teleisha, who has been on long-term sick leave. 'It is Teleisha.'

A multitude of objects on her desk scream their desire to be the first to commence the assault upon its person. Pens, computer monitor, paperweight. Following a deep inhalation, I say, 'I don't want her to be my assistant.'

'Why not?'

'Teleisha is not conscientious and her manner is unprofessional.'

'Tough luck, I'm afraid. We have contractual obligations that must be met. Teleisha is fit to return to work, and that is what will be happening.'

I leave soon after. Teleisha has been absent from the office since the day she claimed she was the victim of harassment during a telephone conversation. That was six months ago. This is a travesty. The KFC-stuffing, personal call-making, work-shy monstrosity is an abomination. Its work habits are about as conducive to the smooth running of Burials and Cemeteries as a resurgence of bubonic plague. Back at my desk, I stab my eraser with a sharpened pencil. If only voodoo were not merely superstition. Asma stands up.

'Is e-everything alright?'

I force a 'Yes.'

Asma should cancel her arranged marriage in Yemen. Her selfish decision has put my department in jeopardy.

It is six-thirty, and I am still toiling at my desk. I get up, go over to the window, and peer out into darkness. In the sky, a satellite is flickering. It resembles a cheap memorial trinket hanging above a gravesite at night, its AA battery on the wane.

FOUR

SECURITY FOR NEWTON BOROUGH'S CEMETERIES was outsourced three years ago to Securicor, one of the country's largest private security firms. Securicor installed top-of-the-range CCTV cameras at all three sites, a project I oversaw personally. Surveillance is a must with cemeteries in this area, as every variety of reprobate with an interest in gaining access to burial grounds is to be found here.

The contract stipulates they must store the previous three months of footage. Yesterday, I got them to send me the CCTV computer files for the duration of the time my target has been employed here. Annoyingly, viewing the files entails installing software, which I have just finished doing. On the desk in front of me are the work schedules for the cemetery maintenance team, stretching back to when Kiro joined the council thirty-seven days ago. This process promises to be irksome and time consuming. If Kiro revealed his left forearm on camera, it would likely to have been at least two weeks ago when the weather was milder.

Presently, I am watching Kiro at the entrance of a cemetery for the fifth day in succession. He is wearing his council-issue coat. I pound my fist on the desk's surface. It is glaringly obvious that if Kiro Burgan is indeed the wanted, alleged war criminal then he would go to great lengths not to reveal his left forearm. Even if temperatures were at Maghreb levels, he would probably still wear long sleeves. And there is always the possibility that he had the tattoo surgically removed, though it would leave considerable scarring, presumably. This prolonged activity has taken up half the day.

Kiro appears to be approximately six foot three. From the footage and pictures on the internet, I am aware that The Wanted One is around the same height as my surly subordinate. I have deduced this due to the fact that my cemetery employee Cheikh is more or less the same height as me, five-eleven. Kiro must be four inches taller than that. I am searching for footage of him on Newton Old's fence line when Darren and housing's Elisa approach my desk. I close the program.

'Alright?' says Darren.

'Good afternoon.'

Elisa prods at Asma's unoccupied desk, and says, 'What do they wear at Halloween, that lot?'

'That lot?'

'*Musers,*' spits Darren.

'Much the same as anyone else presumably. There are no religious stipulations for Muslims concerning Halloween party dress code.'

'White burka, ghost,' says Darren. 'Black burka, Reaper.'

Both laugh at this absurd piece of logic. They wander off; I reopen the program. A figure materialises on the screen. It is Angus arriving at Newton New Cemetery for the early shift. He is wearing a council issue green T-shirt. Come on, be wearing the same. It starts raining. Angus shakes his fists at the heavens. Two coated figures with their hoods pulled up dash past. *Damn!*

A pair of magpies have just landed on the pathway by Boden's entrance. According to a traditional children's nursery rhyme, one magpie is for sorrow, two for joy. Three figures emerge.

'No!'

*

Built in the fifteenth century, Boden Church is the oldest remaining building in the borough. The church was positioned in the middle of Boden Cemetery. However, in the early nineteen-fifties half of the cemetery was built over. It is currently occupied by an Iceland supermarket and a Pound-land. As I am ten minutes early for my meeting with Boden's caretaker, Rebecca, I am enjoying some solitude here. The church is only open at set times of day to the public, times of day I avoid. The rest of the time it is locked up, a result of reprobates congregating here. Heroin addicts use the pews as shooting galleries and drug-addled prostitutes dispense sexual services from the confessional booths. I have my own key.

Although I have no faith in any spurious religious beliefs, I light a prayer candle and watch the flame flicker in the gloom. *Let Kiro Burgan be Darko Draganović.* I amble over to the far wall and inspect a stone sculpture depicting the faces of seven monks. Each of the intricately carved monks exhibits the purported impact of a deadly sin upon his countenance. Wrath, avarice, envy, pride, lust, gluttony, sloth.

Wrath, avarice, envy, pride and lust are really the only emotions there are. It is these so-called sins that have driven some people to evolve and innovate. If they did not exist, people would no doubt still be traveling around on square wheels. How convenient and manipulative it is for the church to label each as a sin. This way whatever a person feels at a given moment is labelled a sin, leaving them riddled with what the church calls guilt. I know what guilt is, but I have never felt it. This makes me sinless for I am aware that I have done no wrong. Sinless people are a threat to the church, as they cannot be subordinated by having sins for Jesus to forgive. As for the Kingdom of Heaven, I would take a mausoleum over it any day of the week.

Sloth and gluttony were invented by the church, to brand anyone a sinner who was opposed to sharing the fruits of their labours with the church in the form of tithes. It is all but irrelevant these days, at least here in Newton Borough, where Christianity has been relegated to third place behind Islam and Sikhism. It would be a sin however if the church's terminal decline resulted in the architecture and art it inspired, such as this example, disappearing. A deadly sin.

I exit the church and head over to Rebecca's residence. It is on the other side of the cemetery. The council-owned property is a perk of the job for the caretaker of Newton's green spaces and outdoor areas. These include parks, play areas, and of course cemeteries. Rebecca opens the door.

'Hi,' she says. 'Punctual as always.'

She ushers me into the kitchen. Her wife, a petite brown-haired woman, is stirring a pot on the stove. She says, 'Hello there.'

I am fairly certain that her name is Karen but it might not be, so I reciprocate with, 'Good evening,' and omit the name.

Their young son *Felix* enters the room. Rebecca says, 'Say hello to our guest, Julian. You remember Dyson.'

'Yes, hi.'

'Hello.'

Rebecca says, 'Drink, Dyson?'

'Yes, please.'

'You've finished work for the day, haven't you?'

'Yes.'

'Whisky then?'

'Why not.'

Before me is a prime example of a modern Newton Borough family unit. Families with same sex parents are everywhere nowadays. Rebecca is conversing with her wife and son. It all seems so fluid, so unapologetic. This is in marked contrast with my own family's embarrassment over my gay father. He was whispered about, but never openly discussed. Only seven people attended his funeral. Rebecca passes me a tumbler with whisky in it. We go into the living room.

'It's a nightmare,' she says. 'At this time of year, with it getting dark so early. There's much to do outside and it all has to be crammed in before dark. Well, what do you want to discuss about the graves then?'

'They are of historical significance. The heritage people will have to be brought in to investigate and provide feedback on the best course of action.'

'Well *yeah*.'

'With any luck the matter can be resolved during a drier time of year. The ground is far too wet now to be dealing with subsidence.'

'That's up to them, isn't it?' She has a sip of whisky. 'Not my problem that.'

'The afflicted headstones are hazardous. If a headstone were to topple on someone's foot, the council could be sued. Have the team cordon off with tape any headstones slanting by more than thirty degrees.'

'Are you expecting me to get the protractor out?'

'I will do the necessary calculations and inform you which are to be cordoned off.'

'Well, there you go then.' I have a sip of whisky. 'Is there anything else?'

'The new cemetery employee.'

'Kiro. He's a knob.'

'In what way?'

'He's pretty punctual, I'll give him that. But has nothing else going for him.'

'Where's he from?'

'From?' She drains her tumbler and plonks it on a coffee table. 'Somewhere beginning with M in Europe. East, or it might be central. It's not Macedonia. Ah.'

'Moldova.'

'Nah.'

'Montenegro.'

'Yeah, that's the one.' She stands up. 'Are we done? Cos if so, I've got stuff to do.'

She takes my empty tumbler. I leave. That was potentially an interesting piece of information. If Kiro is Darko Draganović, it is plausible that he would masquerade as a Montenegrin. After all, Serbian is their traditional language and Montenegro is a historical ally of Serbia, making it the perfect nationality for Darko to adopt.

*

I am being lowered headfirst into a toilet bowl. Beneath its murky water, I can see a coiled turd. To the accompaniment of Beatrice's shrieking laughter, the boys gripping my ankles drop me into the fetid water. I awaken spluttering and writhing about in the bed. Eva places her arm over my chest and coos in my ear, 'What were you dreaming of this time?'

'I wasn't dreaming of anything.'

Having brushed Eva's arm away, I go through to the bathroom and douse my face with cold water. I can hear its grating voice coming from the tap. *Your Daddy died of AIDS, hehe, he. Your Daddy died of AIDS, hehe, he. Your Daddy died of AI–* When I turn the tap off, it stops abruptly. I pat my face dry. In the living room, I collapse on the sofa and take deep breaths through my nose. On the coffee table in front of me there is a small, self-seal transparent plastic bag. The ubiquitous drug storage vessel. I pick it up. It has a green skull printed on one side – the signature of Eva's drug dealer. He goes by the name of Blood something or rather. These green skull-imprinted bags litter the pavement outside my building, as well as my bus stop. I have even come across one in Starbucks. I return to the bedroom to find Eva lying on the bed, propped up on one elbow, a lock of brown hair cascading down over her face. It is evident from her dilated pupils and unruffled hair that she has not slept. When I lie on the bed, she kisses my cheek and rests her head on my shoulder.

Last night, I was watching a report on the news about Royal Mail branch closures when Eva started randomly talking about relationships. She said that men choose women that remind them of their mothers. Over the course of our five-year relationship, Eva has enquired about my mother on a number of occasions. I told her she died when I was young of an illness and left it at that. There appears to be a reasonable chance that Eva will suffer the same fate and die from the effects of drug addiction at a young age.

Doctor Trenton was a smarmy GP in the neighbouring town to where I lived as a child. When I close my eyes, I see my young self stepping into his office. Mother rises from her knees and wipes her mouth with her sleeve. Doctor Trenton hurriedly does up his flies. When we exit the surgery, mother is clutching a bag of multi-coloured pills.

*

The following morning – Voltaire said, *Everything is fine today, that is our illusion.* I am under no illusion. But part of playing the office game is pretending everything is fine. Ultimately, this is to my advantage. It is one of the reasons I rose to become Head of Burials and Cemeteries. As I stroll through the office with my caffè latte extra hot with soya milk, I greet the few council workers who are already here.

'Good morning … Have a great day … Like your new coat … Oh, it's not new.'

HR's Emma is at her desk. It is far too early to hear about her repugnant offspring. I increase my pace. When I pass her desk, I say 'Good morning' and keep walking. Waddling towards me is B-B-B from accounts. 'Good morning.'

'Hi Dyson, how are you?'

'Fine.'

Asma is in early this morning. She says, 'Morning Dyson.'

'Good morning.'

'Nice shirt by the way.'

Yes. It is a slim fit, blue and white, gingham check shirt from Hackett. My in tray looks like a replica of the Leaning Tower of Pisa. It has piled up because I have spent so many hours analysing CCTV footage. While I wait for the computer to turn on, I touch the monocle in my trouser pocket. It used to belong to Doctor Trenton. He came home from the golf course one evening to find me in his house, brandishing a samurai sword. This time it was him on his knees. He pleaded pitifully. I beheaded him and commandeered the monocle.

A plain blonde skips over. It is Amelia, no Andrea, possibly Ann.

'Hey Dyson.'

'Good morning.'

'I was wondering if you were interested in, um, possibly having lunch with me one day later this week. Maybe the new pizza place opposite.' *I was thinking of going there, but not with her.* 'If you're not too busy that is.'

'I am incredibly busy.' The comment is augmented with a tilt of my head in the direction of the Leaning Tower of Pisa in tray. 'As you can see.'

'Oh, well maybe another time?'

I don't respond; she wanders off. After dealing with some emails, I sit tapping my fingertips against the surface of the desk while contemplating the Kiro Burgan situation. On the other side of the passageway to me, some council workers are discussing the forthcoming office Halloween party. This could be a good chance to discover more about him.

'Asma?'

'Yes.'

'Email Rebecca and tell her to invite my two cemetery employees to the office Halloween party. Cheikh and Kiro.'

'But there are three of them.'

'Angus is barred from the building.'

'Really? Why?'

'He got drunk at the Christmas do and sung a Rangers Football Club song with sectarian connotations.'

'Wow!'

The decision to invite them will not be considered unusual. The Halloween party is open to all the council's staff. With alcohol available to loosen his tongue, this event could prove to be an ideal opportunity. He better accept my invitation.

'The wording of your email to Rebecca.'

'What about it?'

'Write that they are expected at the party.'

*

It is lunchtime and I am in a café slash restaurant, sitting amongst the detritus of a once proud nation. Unfortunately, the council periodically organises these lunches as 'an opportunity' for different departments to meet and get to know each other better. I desire to know them less, not better. This meal is for Burials and Cemeteries, the bins department, and the mailroom. Darren leans across the table.

'See your assistant isn't here. Is that cos there's no halal meat on the menu?'

'Asma is working. As she is leaving the council soon, she didn't think there was any point in mingling with other departments.'

'Anti-social that lot are. Stick with their own kind.'

A mobile phone's ringtone on an adjoining table sounds

suspiciously like *The Colour of My Love* by Celine Dion. Its proprietor should be fined for this auditory violation. I put my hands over my ears and focus on the menu ... Will go with a *fettuccine alfredo*. At the other end of the table, Alice is regaling his audience with details of a Guns N' Roses tribute band's concert he went to last weekend. Alice, not his real name, works in the mailroom. I call him Alice because he looks similar to ageing rocker, Alice Cooper. Like the real Alice, he sports a mane of black hair and wizened, heavily lined features. But for record sales read envelopes.

Alice's mailroom colleague, Meagre Martin, is talking. He is virtually devoid of a chin and his face recedes abruptly below his lower lip. If he were a foot or two shorter, he could pass himself off as a primordial dwarf. He is discussing motorbikes with Darren and Alice. Meagre Martin is a biker wannabe, severely restricted by financial constraints. He comes to work on a moped with heightened, Harley Davidson-style handle-bars. A waitress says to me, 'What can I get you?'

'*Fettuccine alfredo* and a Coca-Cola.'

Following a sip of Coca-Cola, I fiddle with the monocle in my trouser pocket. On the other side of the table, bins' supremo Irene, is droning on. She is tubby, bespectacled, drab, and has a mouth that is invariably open. To look upon Irene is to look upon a world of cheap retail outlets, suburban cul-de-sacs, Sky television itineraries, frozen Iceland trifles, and Co-operative Funeralcare plans. Has Rebecca confirmed yet as to whether Kiro will be attending the party? He better be. And if he does, is there any way of getting him to reveal the underside of his left forearm? The food arrives. How disappointing. My *fettuccine alfredo* is about as appetising as Heinz Spaghetti Hoops. Irene is prodding at my plate.

'Is that spaghetti?'

'*Fettuccine alfredo*, purportedly.'

'Purport-edly. Type of sort of sauce that?'

The travesty of justice is that Imbecilic Irene probably earns more than I do. A surge of wrath resonates through my body. On the table, the knives and forks are competing with one another to reflect the sun's rays radiating through the window. They are vying for my attention, willing me to choose them for the imminent assault on bins' head honcho.

*

Two hours later – For the third time this afternoon, I am scanning the Burials and Cemeteries email inbox. On seeing that there is no email from Rebecca, I punch my palm. An email arrives. It has a photograph attached of a garish new memorial bench, which is soon to be deposited at a gravesite at Newton New. The bench is for Mr and Mrs Bowyer. The pair died of food poisoning on a package holiday in Turkey earlier this year. It might have been a salmonella chicken doner that killed them, or maybe a radioactive Turkish delight planted by a Kurdish separatist group, seeking to decimate the country's tourist industry.

A heart-shaped photograph of the couple has been ill-advisedly integrated into the front of the bench. From the couple's grinning faces, it is apparent that the photograph was taken pre-food poisoning. Unfortunately, the bench has the authorised dimensions, or I would ban it. Garish memorial benches should be made an eighth Deadly Sin. An email has arrived. It is from Rebecca. It reads, *Cheikh, Kiro & myself will come. Angus won't obviously.*

FIVE

THE HALLOWEEN PARTY is today. It is fancy dress. Ideally, Kiro will be wearing a short-sleeved outfit that reveals the prominent tattoo on the underside of his left forearm. Of course, if he is the alleged war criminal, he will be keeping the tattoo concealed. Regardless, I will be subtly questioning him about his past. If he lies to me, I will know. I am an expert on body language.

After fastidiously working all morning, my in tray no longer resembles the Leaning Tower of Pisa. It is now two minutes shy of midday, and I am reclining in my revolving office chair looking up at the ceiling. My mobile phone is vibrating. It is Eva. She should not be bothering me at work. I pick it up off the desk and answer it.

'What is it?'

'Come over to mine, quickly.'

'No, I am at work.'

'It's an emergency! Will explain when you get here. Hurry, please.'

She hangs up. How annoying. I say to Asma, 'Have some matters to attend to. I might be a while. Phone me if there are any issues.'

*

As I approach Eva's building, I sip from the cup of caffè latte extra hot with soya milk that I got from Starbucks on the way over. Two twenty-something men in baseball caps are carrying a bed out of the door to Eva's building. The scrawny man at the front has stumpy dreadlocks protruding from the sides of his baseball cap, which is worn backwards. I recognise him as being Eva's drug supplier, Blood something or other. As they pass by me, he flashes a gold-toothed grin.

Eva's front door is on the latch. I find her weeping on the floor in the corner of the kitchen.

'Was that your bed I just saw being carried off?'

She wipes her eyes, mutters, 'Yes.'

'They are collecting drug debts, I presume.' She nods and sobs. 'How much money do you owe?'

She mutters something inaudible. I am poised to repeat my question, when the two men stroll into the kitchen. Blood Whatever points at the kitchen chairs and claps. His accomplice proceeds to pick up two chairs. Blood Whatever says to Eva, 'Woman, who's dat?'

'My boyfriend!' blurts Eva, who now clambers up to her feet.

I say, 'How much is her debt?'

'Dire.'

'That is not a number.' When I take out my wallet, he clicks his fingers, and the accomplice lowers the chairs. He is grinning again, revealing gold-capped teeth. 'Well?'

'Two grand.'

I say, 'Seriously Eva?'

'I'm sorry, it got out of control.'

'Wholly irresponsible.'

'I know that!'

I extract sixty pounds from my wallet. The accomplice laughs maniacally. Blood Whatever says, 'Nah, a monkey.'

'Excuse me?'

'Monkey I said. You deaf?'

42

'I am not an illegal wildlife trader.'

Blood Whatever throws his arm up, and his accomplice says, 'Are you for real?'

'A monkey,' screeches Eva, 'is five-hundred pounds!'

She resumes sobbing. Having snatched the banknotes off me, Blood Whatever orders his accomplice to take one of the chairs. The accomplice drags a chair over to the door. Blood Whatever says, 'Two grand ASAP.' He stares at Eva who is cowering in the corner. 'No pay, gang rape or go to sleep.'

The remark is augmented with a thrust of his hips followed by a finger drawn across his throat. I say, 'This is unreasonable. You've taken a bed, a chair and sixty pounds. One thousand seven hundred is her outstanding debt. That is my final offer.'

'Nah fool,' he says. 'Interest.'

'Preposterous.'

Eva holds her palms out, and shrieks, 'Leave it, Dyson!'

When I take a step towards Blood Whatever, he lifts his tracksuit top, revealing the stock of a handgun tucked into the waistband of his tracksuit bottoms. Eva gasps. The stock has coloured horizontal bands engrained on it. They are green, white and blue, the colours of the Sierra Leone flag. The pair leave and slam the front door behind them. Eva is weeping. I crouch down in front of her.

'This is ridiculous. How could you have got in this situation? You shouldn't have had any dealings in the first place with that imbecile, Blood Whatever.'

'Blood Letz.'

'Letz?'

'Yes, Letz.' She wipes her eyes with her forearm. 'Letz means blood out.'

'He's not Austrian then?'

'Of course not!' Her neck cranes forward. 'You're not even scared, you're making jokes. You're a psychopath.'

How ungrateful. If it wasn't for me, she would have no

43

chairs left and other furniture would likely have been taken to. And I forked out sixty pounds. Eva slumps sobbing to the floor. People often react by blaming others in these kinds of situations. Only last week, I watched a programme about a man who killed a postman and blamed his mother for it.

Strewn across the kitchen worktop are bills. These include an overdue television licence fee letter and a final demand for payment for an electricity bill. The living room, which not long ago was congested with furniture, is all but empty. Only a solitary bookshelf remains, virtually bereft of books. This place, and most of what is, or rather was in it, belongs to Eva's parents. When they moved back to Croatia last year, they let her stay on here. In the kitchen, Eva tilts her tear-streaked face up at me, and says, 'You don't care.'

'I do care, I saved your chair. And paid a first instalment on your debt.' I look down at her. 'Don't let those two back in here.' She nods multiple times, the movements small but rapid. 'I will pay off your debt.' She grips my trouser leg. 'On the condition that you get your drug issue under control.' Further nods. I pull my leg free. 'I am returning to work.'

'Already?'

'Yes, I have money to earn. I've spent sixty pounds this lunchbreak and I haven't even bought a sandwich yet.'

*

At the office, I take the monocle from my drawer and rotate it in my fingertips, remembering as I do so the fate of the last man who plied someone associated to me with drugs. The afternoon is spent grappling with the in tray. By five o'clock it is clear who the winner is. I rub my palms together. This evening I will be focusing solely on Kiro and will not be devoting any thought to the drug dealing reprobate with the Austrian-esque name.

44

'Goodbye Asma. I will see you later at the party. Sterling work today by the way.'

'Thank you. See you later.'

I go home to collect my Halloween outfit. On the way Frank texts me, enquiring as to whether I am available for a pre-party drink. No, there is not enough time. Eva telephones me. She says that she is with friends who are *caring for* her, and that she is sorry for everything and grateful for my help. That is more like it.

After collecting the outfit, I make my way to Newton Old Cemetery with the gym bag containing the outfit swinging by my side. I unlock the gate's padlock and enter the premises. The cemetery is a square plot, measuring a little over a third of an acre. It is surrounded by moss-ridden walls and is densely clustered with seventeenth century graves. The deceased who are interred here are all victims of the Great Plague of London. These suburban Londoners were well off enough to avoid the communal lime pits. What with it being the end of October, it is already dark. I switch on my torch and weave between the graves to the small shed on the far side of the graveyard. I locate the key on my keyring and unlock the padlock. On a shelf is the mini chainsaw that is used by the maintenance team to prune branches here. Having wrapped the chainsaw in a bin liner, I place it in the gym bag.

At the council, I ascend to floor five where I change in a cubicle in the men's toilets, and then inspect my reflection in the mirrors above the basins. Staring at me is a worn, brown leather mask, with crudely fashioned holes for the eyes and mouth. I am wearing a white cotton shirt and an apron, which is heavily stained with dark red dye. A black tie, not the python one, rests atop of it. In one hand I am holding the chainsaw, the blade now smeared with blood red dye. In the other, I have a life-sized, rubber human head.

For quite some time I admire this exact replica of Leatherface, the character from the iconic 1974 horror movie, *The Texas*

Chainsaw Massacre. The head is artistic licence on my part. I previously wore this outfit to a Halloween bash at someone's house. I received compliments all night long. No one's outfit will compare to this. Right, time to discover more about the mysterious Kiro.

When the lift door opens, I see that floor nine's ceiling is covered in pumpkin-shaped balloons. I step out of the lift. A child stops feverishly licking at a toffee apple on a stick, and gapes at me.

'WAHHH!' It spins around and scampers off at quite a pace in the direction of the party attendees, who are gathered at the far end of the open-plan office. 'MUMMY!'

As I advance through the office, faces turn to me. Many of their mouths are open. It is the usual Halloween meets council workers scene. Witches in cloaks and demons with horned headbands and plastic pitchforks. Two finance workers hold *Scream* film series-inspired ghost masks to their faces and make ghoul-like noises. The children surrounding them squeal. When the children look at me, the squeals become shrieks. Cheikh has come as a red-caped demon. Rebecca is wearing fangs and a cloak. Her child stares at me as he clings to her leg. Rebecca is holding her middle finger out at me. What atrocious manners. There is no sign of Kiro.

A mixed-race witch is strutting towards me. She has a firm grip on the wrist of the child who made the *WAHHH!* noise. She works in sport, leisure and culture, and is shapely and fairly attractive.

'Oi, what are you thinking, scaring my child like that?'

'Halloween is supposed to be scary.'

'You've gone way overboard.'

A pumpkin approaches. The head comes off, revealing Sunita. It growls, 'Rakesha, I'll deal with him.' Mother and child wander off. 'That thing better not be real?' It prods at the mini chainsaw. 'It is, isn't it? What were you thinking?'

'As you can see, the teeth have a rubber protective cover over them.'

It *snorts*, passes me a key, and says, 'Lock it in the stationery cupboard. Oh, and that ghastly thing too. That has no place here. Go!'

It struts off. How dare it try to humiliate me? That *bindi* dot better tremor and the back of its head explode soon. Without my accessories, I look like a butcher shop worker. This is an outrage. Having placed the chainsaw and head in the stationery cupboard, I give it a kick and return to the party. Kiro still isn't here.

I help myself to a glass of subpar plonk masquerading as red wine. Darren and Frank are dressed as characters from *The Addams Family*. Darren is Uncle Fester. He has shaved his head, is wearing black eyeliner and is clad in a black coat. Frank is supposed to be the tall, Frankenstein-esque character. However, it is ineffective as he is of average height. Frank says, 'Dyson, that was some entrance.'

'Ill 'un you are,' says Darren. He gestures with a jut of his chin at Rebecca. 'Check aht the vampire strap-on queen.'

He is evidently already drunk. Asma walks over. She is dressed as a black cat. Ears are attached to the top of her veil and a tail is pinned to her posterior.

'Hi Dyson.'

'Good evening, Asma.'

She moves away. Darren says, 'So she poles up to this but not the lunch. Do as they please over here those musers.'

Frank nudges Darren's shoulder, and says, 'Tone it down.'

'Alright. Fuckin' 'ell!'

Where is Kiro? A girl, probably finance, totters past in a skimpy, mini-skirted demon outfit. Darren shoots off after her. Oh no, here comes Imbecilic Irene in a vampire meets Worzel Gummidge outfit. She says, 'Hi, Dyson.'

'Good evening.'

47

'Hear you've been a naughty boy.'

Go away. She waddles off. That's better. The girl Darren pursued is gesticulating wildly at him. Having hurried over to me, he prods at a man with his back to us wrapped in a sheet, that has not seen the laundry in quite some time.

'Who's that cunt? A fuckin' refugee?'

Frank says, 'He didn't exactly pull the stops out.'

It could be Kiro ... It is Kiro. I amble over to him, and say, 'Good evening, Kiro.'

'Hi.'

'All well with you?'

He shrugs his hefty shoulders, and says, 'Not bad.' So Kiro has come as a tramp, a miserable one at. 'What're you looking at?'

'Your outfit.'

'Ghost, okay. You, butcher shop worker.' *Ahh!* 'How is that Halloween, eh?'

'I had accessories.'

'Accessories?'

'Yes, a mini chainsaw and head.'

'Haha, a real sicko.'

'Excuse me?'

'Ha, ha.'

Impertinent man. I am his superior. Up close he looks the spitting image of the war criminal Darko, if he were fifteen years older.

'How is work?'

Again, he shrugs his shoulders. He says, 'Done better, done worse.'

'What were you doing previously, prior to joining my team?'

'Your team?' A thick finger extends. 'If your team, where are you when we are working in the wet, in the cold?'

'Running operations from the office.'

'Indoors, huh. Easy.'

'Actually, my work is rather complex.' What an ignorant and disrespectful lout. His forearms are completely covered by the fetid sheet, making identification impossible. If he is capable of this sort of base behaviour, he could have a penchant for ethnic cleansing. He downs his glass of wine. 'What is it that you were doing prior to coming here?'

'Want to know ask the employment agency you used to hire me.'

'Well, I'm asking you. I am making conversation.'

Following a grunt, he says, 'Sewage work in Sheffield.'

'How was the work?'

'It was sewage, how do you think it was?'

He pulls the sheet over him and stomps off. I am poised to pursue him when housing's drunken Elisa bumps into me. Her dumpy physique is clad in black PVC. She resembles a black bin liner bulging with rubbish.

'What did you do with your chainsaw and head.'

'They have been put away for now.'

But if you don't leave me alone, I will get that chainsaw and ... She drags her gnawed, purple-painted fingernails across the front of my fake blood-stained apron. If this is seduction, it is the depths of it. Kiro has disappeared.

*

The next morning – I am re-familiarising myself with the financial software package, Sage. As Asma is soon to be replaced by the workshy monstrosity that is Teleisha, it is apparent that Sage-related matters will be my sole responsibility. The email icon flashes on my screen. It is from Sunita, informing me that I am fortunate not to be facing disciplinary measures, and that chainsaws indoors with children and alcohol present breach a host of health and safety regulations.

49

Preposterous. It was a mini chainsaw, and it didn't even have fuel in it. Darren materialises by my desk. He glowers at Asma, mutters something inaudible, then says, 'I'm in big shit. Some of the birds at the party complained I was tryin' to get in their pants. Just a bit of banter. Cunts!'

He saunters off. Asma is shaking her head. Here comes sport, leisure and culture's boss Grace and her colleague Rakesha. I say, 'Good morning.'

'Don't you be good morning me!' says Rakesha, whose fists are on her hips.

'What were you thinking terrifying those little children like that?' chimes in Grace.

'My daughter had nightmares about you.'

'Explain yourself?'

There is no advantage to be had in confronting this ludicrous pair. I say, 'Unfortunately, I was not told little children were going to be present.'

'How could you not know?' says Rakesha. 'Everyone knew.'

'It was not something that was discussed in my department. Besides, I didn't attend the Halloween party last year or the year before, as I was away. The last time I did, no small children were present.'

'They were this time,' says Grace.

'Indeed. And on discovering they were, I immediately modified my outfit to take them into account. By the way, Rakesha, you have a beautiful daughter. I can see where she gets her looks from.'

Rakesha takes her fists off her hips, and says, 'Thank you.'

Grace blows air from her mouth, and says, 'Let's get going.'

They wander off. Rakesha swivels her head and looks at me. I wink at her. The next task is to integrate my Excel financial forecasting reports into Sage … Easy. Frank strolls up to my desk. I say, 'Good morning.'

'Quick chat.' He tilts his neck to the side. 'Outside.'

'Not now, I am busy re-familiarising myself with Sage.'

He leans over me and says, 'Let's go, Dyson.' I follow him out of the office to the stairwell. 'Chainsaw at an office Halloween party. Bad idea.'

'Mini chainsaw.'

'Chainsaw nonetheless. Sharp, heavy, dangerous. What were you thinking? The world has gone way overboard with health and safety, as you know as well as anyone … Chainsaws, even mini chainsaws, belong outdoors or in a shed. End of. The whole council agrees on this, trust me.'

'The mini chainsaw had a protective cover over the blade, so it couldn't cut anything. My Halloween-inspired outfit was superb. It was original and scary.'

'Your outfit was scary, yes. It was also disturbing.' He passes his palm across his thinning hair. 'A Halloween party, well an office Halloween party anyway, is an opportunity to entertain and socialise with your fellow colleagues, within, err, socially acceptable parameters. *The Texas Chainsaw Massacre* is one of the scariest films ever made, period. Okay, it's pretty dated. But it's harrowing stuff. Saw it in my teens. Darren's Dad had it on video … The only good thing was Emma wasn't there. Because if her precious kid had seen you, she would have had a heart attack.'

'This is not a big deal.'

'Not now it's not, because I persuaded Sunita to let it go.' He sighs. 'Darren's another matter.' Frank places his arm around my neck and squeezes. 'Think before you act. And if in doubt, ask.'

I'm never in doubt.

SIX

TWO DAYS LATER – As I ruminate on the Kiro Burgan issue, I tap the base of my pen against the desk. There is a report in my in tray from a local think tank, outlining the projected rate of deaths in the borough over the forthcoming decade. It proves to be interesting and informative. After several minutes spent scrutinising the data, my thoughts turn to Kiro once more. Affirmative action must be taken. All I need is a glance at his left forearm, so I can either discount him, or pursue the reward. Asma calls out from her desk, 'A-a body's been found, a possible public funeral case, the police are there.' The day is looking up. She is waving her handset in the air. 'Fraser is on the line.'

'Put him through … Good morning.'

'Dyson, tried your mobile but you didn't answer.'

'It's on silent mode, I just came out of a meeting.'

'There's a body, public funeral case it appears. Can you go to the address and do the honours? I'm stuck at a wake. Will meet you there, shouldn't be too long. Here's the address …'

'I will get over there right away.'

'See you there.'

Cranley Gardens is approximately twenty seconds' walk from my residence. The place is infamous for a tuberculosis outbreak there a few years ago. I grab the suit jacket off the back of my chair.

'Asma, you're in charge. Don't let Darren near my desk.'

There is no sign of the lift so I will take the stairs. Being out in the field is the best part of the job. Unfortunately, it doesn't happen very often. Due to budget cuts, police will only stay at the scene of a death that is not a suspected murder, or in a public place, for more than twenty minutes. This is because they are required elsewhere. In the instance of a suspected public funeral case (i.e. where there are no known next of kin or relatives) the scene is secured, scrutinised, and the public funeral contractor contacted. Fraser in Newton Borough instances. However, when Fraser is busy, I fill the void. This is only the sixth time there has been such an occurrence in the last three years.

I am in a mini cab. What is the driver doing?

'Why didn't you turn right there?'

'I forgot.'

'Do a U-turn.' My mobile is ringing. It is Fraser. 'Hello.'

'Going to be longer than I thought. Get one of your guys to help.'

He hangs up. It has to be someone with a Level 4B certificate that covers hazardous waste and cadavers. Cheikh is my only employee who is in possession of one. Unless Kiro has a Level 4B. Picking up a body could be the perfect opportunity to get him to roll up his sleeves and reveal his left forearm. I telephone Rebecca. After several rings, she answers.

'*Ha* Dyson, chainsaw and a severed head, wh—'

'Rebecca, I require assistance with a body and time is of the essence. By any chance does Kiro Burgan have a Level 4B certificate?'

'Doubt it. Cheikh has a 4B, thought you knew that. He's about, I think. Give him a bell. Here's his number ...' *What is this driver doing?* 'Pull in over there on the left.'

I disembark, telephone Cheikh and give him the address. He says he will be twenty minutes. I bundle into the building behind an old woman dragging a wheeled shopping trolley, then race up the stairs. En route to floor four, I brush past a group of teenagers smoking weed and conversing in a South Asian language. A policeman is outside the flat. I flash my Council ID. He says, 'A travel card don't get you entry.'

'This is my Burials and Cemeteries ID card. I am the Head ...'

'He's alright,' comes a voice from inside. A policewoman exits the flat. I saw her at the last incident of this nature I attended. 'All yours, enjoy. Oh, and lock the door from the inside until your back-up gets here.'

The sound of static on the policewoman's radio is followed by, 'Youths ransacking Foot Locker on the high road, over.'

The pair rush off. Inside the flat, there is the distinctive aroma of death. I press a light switch on the wall. Nothing happens. The only source of illumination in here are the shards of light, penetrating through gaps around the boarded-up windows. Strips of tattered wallpaper hang from the fungus-blotched walls. Somewhere a bluebottle is buzzing listlessly. The room's only piece of furniture is a decrepit sofa covered in holes. The body is behind the sofa, lying contorted on its back with its head slanted to one side. Straggly, greasy brown hair hangs over skeletal features. It has bulging eyes and a black, ulcer-ridden tongue protruding from an open mouth that houses chipped, stained rodent teeth.

When I crouch beside it, the pungent odour emanating from the corpse's pants grows more potent. On pulling down the collar of its moth-eaten sweater, it is apparent from the emaciated throat's Adam's apple that it was male, deeming further explorations unnecessary. In the latter stages of some drug addictions the difference between the genders rescinds, bringing them closer together than any piece of gender equality-based legislation.

I am in control of his fate. One press of a button and this degenerate goes to the cremator to the sound of Celine Dion's dismal wails. His ashes will be interred in the section of the wall in Newton New's cremation area, reserved for public funeral cases. Unless of course a relative can be found who is prepared to pay for a plot. It is highly unlikely anyone will want to associate themselves with what lies before me.

While I wait for Cheikh and Fraser to arrive, I have a look around the property. The aged, ragged carpet has been pulled from the floor and lies discarded in lengths around the rooms' edges, presumably to be used as blankets by squatting addicts. In the kitchen, a scuttling rat topples over empty Pot Noodle containers like skittles. The bathroom contains a spattered toilet, devoid of a seat and surrounded by newspaper, soiled with excrement. Scattered across the floor are syringes, paper wraps and small, transparent seal bags. I pick up one of the bags. It has the familiar green skull printed on it. Not only has Blood Letz plied my girlfriend with debt, but he is also spending my department's budget on his victims' public funerals. Now this is getting personal.

There is a knock at the door. Fraser and Cheikh are on the other side, holding a stretcher and some covers between them. Fraser says, 'Ran into each other on the way up here. Thought he looked like one of yours.'

Cheikh says, '*Bonjour.*'

'Good morning.'

While peering at the corpse, Fraser says, 'Nothing like the smell of a skag addict's post-mortem defecation. Its last act of ignominy.'

Cheikh and Fraser are strapping the covered body to the stretcher. Having opened the door for them, I lead the way.

'Dyson, you ever tell Cheikh about the dead druggie in that squat?'

'No.'

'Will never forget it. It was a scene straight out of the film, *The Mummy.*'

'*The Mummy*?' says Cheikh.

I say, '*La Momie.*'

'Ah *oui*, Brendan Fraser *et* Rachel Weisz.'

'But instead of locusts,' says Fraser, 'it was swarming flies.'

'Locusts?' says Cheikh.

'*Sauterelles*,' says I.

'And swarming?'

'*Volée*,' says Fraser.

'*Grouillement* is more apt.'

The teenagers smoking on the stairwell shove their noses under their tops and flee. Despite the cold the hearse windows remain wound down on the way to the parlour. At Raven & Co., the body is dumped in the mortuary fridge. Fraser's secretary asks if I can stay for tea. I am going to use this opportunity to pry Cheikh for information on Kiro, so I decline.

I go to McDonalds with Cheikh. I order a small Coca-Cola and two cheeseburgers for myself and the same for him. He takes out his timesheet. I look at my watch, do a quick calculation, and say, 'One hour forty minutes. I will put two hours.'

'*Merci.*'

While we eat, we converse in French. Cheikh admits to being somewhat perturbed by what he perceives as Fraser's lack of respect for the dead. Cheikh, it transpires, hails from the Democratic Republic of the Congo. He fled his homeland during the Second Congo War and went to Belgium before moving to the UK. Cheikh says his parents and siblings were slain by Rwandan-backed rebels. Having discarded a pickle from my second cheeseburger, I say, 'How is work going?'

'It's going well, I like the job. The weather not so much.'

'That is the UK for you, especially at this time of year. How is your new colleague Kiro fitting into the team?'

Cheikh sighs, and says, 'So, so.'

'Maybe he just needs some time to settle in. Kiro is Montenegrin, isn't he?'

'Don't know. We don't speak much.'

He changes the subject. I subtly steer the conversation back to Kiro, but he has nothing more to add. Cheikh says that he is trying to overcome the loss of his family. I look at my watch.

*

The next day – I am all about creating opportunities. This is one of the many reasons that I was promoted to Head of Burials and Cemeteries. Newton New's crematorium and chapel caretaker Simeon telephoned earlier, to tell me in intricate detail about the cremator that is being installed. My plan is to use the dead addict's public funeral as the cremator's christening-slash-team-get-together. I will check my cemetery maintenance team's schedule ... They are working in Newton New next Tuesday and finish at four.

I telephone Simeon and provisionally book the cremator for next Tuesday at three. I then contact Fraser. He tells me the day and time is convenient for him. Excellent. The body has not been identified, so there is virtually no risk now of anyone organising a private funeral. It is abundantly clear that Kiro Burgan is not a garrulous creature. If he is Darko Draganović, he will not be inadvertently revealing the fact. I must get Kiro to expose the underside of his left forearm during the event. But how? Informing my team it is to be a short-sleeved event could arouse suspicion, if my sullen employee is the alleged war criminal he resembles so closely. Angus' telephone number is in the database. I will call him and inform him of the party plans. There is no need for Rebecca to attend.

Darren and Elisa materialise next to my desk. Elisa says, 'We're discussing our favourite songs, Dyson.'

'Good for you.'

She says, 'No need to be sarky.'

Discourteous council worker.

'That's Dyson for yah.'

Elisa says, 'You might be a bit more enthusiastic, Dyson, if we discuss funeral songs. My favourite's Frank Sinatra's *My Way*.'

'Fuck off!' says Darren.

I say, '*My Way* is tolerable.'

Meagre Martin deposits some mail in my in tray. Elisa says to him, 'Martin, we're discussing our favourite funeral songs?'

'Oh yeah!'

Elisa says, 'Darren, your turn?'

'Can't think of any. Can tell you what I fuckin' hate at a funeral. What they played at Dorothy's. A Celine Dion number.'

'Do not mention that name again in my department.'

'Take it, Dyson, you don't like her music much,' says Elisa. 'What's your fave anyway?'

'Chopin's *Funeral March*.'

'Wanker,' says Darren.

'You miserable sod,' says Elisa.

Insolent imbeciles. 'Evidently you don't have work to do, but I do.'

Elisa says, 'Martin?'

'Yeah.'

'You're being very quiet. What's your fave funeral song?'

Having tapped a knuckle against his non-existent chin, Meagre Martin says, 'Something by Metallica.'

'Now we're talking.'

Darren says, 'Yeah, Metallica's alright.'

'Metallica is not appropriate funeral music,' I point out.

'Says who?' enquires Elisa.

'Me.'

Meagre Martin's mailroom colleague Alice is carrying a parcel through the office. Elisa calls out to him, 'What's your favourite funeral song.'

'*Long Way To the Top* by AC/DC.'

'Wicked song,' says Darren.

'Love *Long Way to the Top*,' says Elisa.

Meagre Martin pretends he is holding a microphone to his mouth. He sings, 'Ridin' down the highway. Goin' to a show. Stop in all the byways. Playin' rock 'n roll …'

Alice and Darren fall to their knees and play air guitar. Meanwhile Elisa laughs maniacally. I recline in my chair and watch the bizarre spectacle. Finance's supremo strides over.

'Come on you lot, get back to work.'

Everyone leaves. I could either order my cemetery employees to remove their coats, or turn up the heating to ensure that they take off their coats. However, if he is not wearing his council-issue T-shirt or another short-sleeved garment, this will prove futile. I smash my fist on the desk. Asma, who has just returned to her desk, says, 'Is everything okay, Dyson?'

'Yes.'

Friday is her last day. My mobile phone is vibrating. It is Eva. I pick up the device, leave the office, go into the stairwell, and answer it.

'Hello Eva.'

'Blood Letz is hassling me. Keeps phoning and someone's been knocking at my door. I haven't got any money at the moment and no one else to turn to.' Through the glass pane in the fire door, I can see Rakesha bending over a printer. Her shapely, skirted posterior is aimed in my direction. 'You did say you'd rectify this matter. They were your exact words. Please pay him something, even just a little bit to keep him off my back. I'm so sorry to ask. Will reimburse you, I promise. Please!'

'Text me his number and I will arrange to make a payment.'

'Thank you. I'll do it right aw—'

I hang up. On re-entering the office, Rakesha says, 'You were looking at me.'

'Yes.' I wink at her. 'Was admiring the view.'

She smiles, twirls a strand of curly brown hair in her fingertip, and says, 'Nice to see you too. How's everything?'

'Everything is fine.'

'Pleased to hear it.' She frowns. 'Having a nightmare with this printer. Paper keeps jamming. Timing couldn't be worse. Got to get copies of this lot done.' She waves a wad of papers in the air. 'For a meeting in half an hour.'

'I will assist you.'

'Oh, thank you that's so kind.' I am an expert at trouble shooting printer problems. It transpires that paper is jamming in tray two. Within a minute I have fixed the issue. 'Done it already? You're amazing.'

'A pleasure.' I scan her shapely figure. 'Let me know if you have any more problems with the printer.'

'Will do.'

*

That evening – I am on my way to a rendezvous with Blood Letz. There he is, surrounded by a posse, below the railway arches on an illuminated skateboard ramp. There are two teenage girls, his male accomplice from last time, and a large mastiff. As I draw closer to the group, the dog barks frenziedly and pulls on its chain. The girl holding the chain is dragged through the dirt towards me. She screeches, 'Easy Cannibal!'

'Rah, rah, rah …'

Foam is spilling from its jaws. The other girl grabs the chain. Having given the dog a wide berth, I approach the ramp, on top of which the two young men are perched.

'Yo!' shouts Blood Letz. 'Where's the money at, bitch?'

'I have it with me.' He will pay for his impertinence. Blood Letz reaches down and clicks his fingers. From the inside pocket of my suit jacket, I extract a wad of twenty-pound notes and hold them up to him. He snatches them. 'Two hundred pounds there.' He counts the money. 'I will have more for you soon.'

'Better.'

The dog has finally stopped barking. One of the girls says to me, 'You're fit.'

The other says, 'James Bond you are.'

I can accept that comparison.

'Shut it hoes!' shouts Blood Letz. He leaps off the skateboard ramp and stands facing me. What a meagre specimen. 'Fuck off!' There is a stumpy dreadlock on the front of his head entwined with yellow, green and red cotton. That dreadlock will be my memento. 'You deaf? Told you already, fuck off!'

*

The following Tuesday – Fraser is pacing in circles across the mortuary floor. With his white apron and his usually gelled back hair a matted mess, he resembles a mad scientist. His secretary is standing next to me in the mortuary's doorway. She says, 'He's gone completely mad, never seen him this bad.'

She re-enters the office area. I step into the mortuary. A cheap MDF-veneered casket is on the floor. It must be the dead drug addict's. Fraser spins around and exclaims, 'Hey, Dyson! What's up?' He leans over the mortuary slab and proceeds to *snort* a white-powdered substance. 'Absolute cack. But does the job if you do enough of it.' *This is neither the time nor the place for the consumption of recreational drugs.* He resumes pacing. 'You don't approve Dyson, I can tell. What do you expect though with the company I keep?'

Fraser kicks the MDF-veneered casket, leaving a dent in the side of it. The secretary appears in the doorway.

'Fraser!'

He stops pacing, and says, 'What, Sally?'

'Mr Pilkington's on the phone, he wants to speak to you about Friday.'

'HA HA!' laughs Fraser. 'That is truly remarkable, Mr Pilkington phoning up when he died last week.'

'That was Mrs Pilkington.'

'Oh.' Fraser collapses in a chair and wipes his face with his palms. 'Tell him I'm at a funeral and will phone him tomorrow.'

She leaves. On a shelf there are three bottles of red wine. There are biscuits and orange squash at the venue. However, alcohol could be a more effective way to keep the maintenance team hanging around.

'Fraser, those bottles of red wine over there.'

'What of them?'

'We and the team could drink them after the christening of the new cremator.'

'The hundred-pound bottles of Burgundy Mrs Rosovsky gave me as a gift for embalming her husband. You're suggesting sharing them with those reprobates, Simeon and Co. Jesus Christ! Go on then.'

*

We are in the hearse, travelling at considerable speed. Fraser spins the steering wheel, we swerve around a corner, and the casket crashes against the side of the vehicle. Fraser bellows 'WOAH!' and pounds his fists on the dashboard. Now we are moving not much faster than walking speed. The cars behind us *beep* their horns. Fraser winds down the window, extends his arm through it and raises his middle finger. The *beeping* intensifies. There are shouted obscenities too, in various languages. The objective today is to get a peek at Kiro's left forearm, not cause a road-rage incident.

At traffic lights, Fraser opens a paper wrap and sticks his nose in it. *Snort!* The lights have turned green and cars are sounding their horns. He stamps on the accelerator. The hearse screeches to a halt at traffic lights on Newton High Street. Two young women are padding along the pavement. Fraser unwinds my window, leans across me, and shouts, 'Hey honey, fancy a ride?'

'Nah, you're gross.'

'Not you, Ugly. Was speaking to your fit friend. Only way I'd give you a ride would be if you were in the back.'

'Sick bastard!'

Fraser roars with laughter. The lights change and the hearse lurches forward. Fraser selecting today for a mental breakdown is most unhelpful. I bow my head. The bottles of burgundy are in a bag at my feet. Red wine stains clothes. I am thrown backwards as the hearse careens along the road. Fraser steps on the brake pedal and spins the steering wheel. We skid across the road as an incoming moped swerves out of the way. Having narrowly avoided a stone pillar at the entrance to Newton New, Fraser bangs his forehead on the steering wheel, and screams, 'YEAH!'

He proceeds to drive through Newton New Cemetery at fifty miles an hour. I shout 'STOP!'

'WOAH!'

He slams his foot on the brake pedal, the hearse veers across the path, bounces off a heart-shaped gravestone, and bumps to a halt. I grip Fraser by his collar.

'You're here to conduct a funeral, not take the Head of Burials and Cemeteries on a roller-coaster-cum-grave vandalising ride.'

I release my grip. Fraser looks down and stammers, 'M-my wife had a miscarriage and I-I don't know what to do. E-everything's gone wrong.'

He starts sobbing. I disembark. First Eva, now him. These drug-crazed histrionics are becoming tedious. One of the hearse's front lights is smashed and the fender is severely scratched. Unfortunately, the heart-shaped gravestone is unscathed. Forty metres or so away in the cremation area, two faces are turned towards me. It is Cheikh and Angus. Where is he?

I scour the gravestone, headstone, memorial bench, and Essex cherub-clustered terrain. A teenage mother is pushing a pushchair along the path. A person slouched on a memorial bench is drinking from a can of cider. Positioned beside an Essex cherub is a man with his back to me. He pivots around and does up his flies. It is him. Good. Having spilled Burgundy on his left sleeve, I will instil a sense of urgency. Salt dabbed with water is supposed to be effective in removing red wine stains. I will say, *Roll down your sleeve and sprinkle salt on it, then dab it with water. Here is some salt.* There better be salt in there, otherwise water will have to suffice.

Fraser is inspecting the front of the hearse. He wipes his eyes, and says, 'Could be worse.'

When I enter the chapel, Simeon scurries over to me. His shirt is untucked, lengths of grey hair are sticking out haphazardly from his balding pate, and he is clutching the new cremator's manual.

'The CT III cremates sixty-five kilograms per hour. Zero mercury emissions and it's compliant with every country's environmental policy, even Japan and Fin—'

'I will be with you in a minute.'

I go through to the funeral hall adjoining the chapel, where Dorothy's repast refreshments were served and where today's post-cremation session will be. I turn the heating dial up. With any luck this will persuade Kiro to take off his upper body garments, other than the council issue T-shirt he will hopefully be wearing underneath. A Burgundy spillage is my back-up plan. The tattoo better be there. That one point five million Euro reward for Darko's capture would come in extremely useful.

Me, Simeon and Fraser pull the casket from the hearse, hoist it up and carry it through to the cremation room. There is to be no funeral service today. Inside, the casket is placed on a trolley. The new cremator is a sleek, steel structure that looks like an elongated microwave with a chimney. Searing flames are visible through the window in its hatch. Fraser says, 'This CT III is infinitely more streamline than the Belcher Mark I contraption you had in here.'

'The CT III is the best!' exclaims Simeon. He bounds over to a computer, wipes his nose on the sleeve of his shirt then feverishly taps keys on the computer's keyboard. While he does so, I look over his shoulder. The password he just entered is the same as it has always been. Ashes2Ashes69. 'Give me the weight and name of the deceased.'

'Fifty-seven kilos,' says Fraser.

'Ignōtus B313,' says I.

Ignōtus is Latin for unknown. Here in Newton Borough all male public funeral cases are designated the name Ignōtus and a four-digit alphanumerical code. This was my idea. I watch Simeon press buttons on the cremator's control panel. A light above the cremator turns green and the hatch opens. Me and Simeon wheel the trolley forward and push the casket into the cremator. The door closes and the casket is engulfed in flames.

Everyone moves to the cremator observation room. A cream-textured leather sofa and chairs surround a large, flat screen television attached to the wall. When Simeon switches it on, a raging furnace appears on the screen. Simeon opens a rusted Quality Street box. Inside are custard creams, no doubt leftovers from a funeral repast, which he offers to me and Fraser. We decline. The casket collapses and the desiccated cadaver rapidly disintegrates in the searing heat. Simeon rubs his palms together, and says, 'Hope there's a treat.'

Simeon is referring to cobalt-chromium, titanium and nickel. These metals are used for hip and knee replacements. Simeon flogs them to scrap yards. We go to the cremator room. Having probed the red-hot cremains, he says, 'Nothing big in there. Could be some fillings though.'

The remains will be left for a short while before being crushed by the cremulator. The hot ash will then continue cooling for another twenty-four hours. Tomorrow, I will return with the priest and an official mourner and collect the ashes. A five-minute service will be conducted in the cremation area. It is almost four o'clock. I cross my fingers. When we go through to the funeral hall, Fraser says, 'It's as hot as the cremator in here.' Simeon turns down the heating. 'I'll go get the Burgundy.'

Angus and Cheikh enter the hall. Where is he? Cheikh says, 'Good afternoon.'

'Hoat!' says Angus. 'Tops off.'

Angus peels off his coat and a Rangers Football Club top underneath which he is sporting a green, council-issue T-shirt. Cheikh removes his coat, scarf and jumper. He is also wearing a council-issue T-shirt. When Kiro lumbers into the hall, I say, 'Good afternoon.'

Kiro reciprocates with a grunted, 'Hey.'

He proceeds to haul off his coat and jumper, revealing a long-sleeved garment. *Ahh!* Plan B. I address the gathering.

'Welcome everyone. Cheikh, Angus, Kiro, you have done a good job. My cemeteries look impeccable. The work you three have put in clearing up the leaves has been first-rate.'

'Ya belter!' exclaims Angus. 'The big man's happy.'

Kiro yawns. *Outrageous manners.* Fraser comes in. The bottles of Burgundy are cradled in his arms. Angus shouts, 'Here comes the cheeky water!'

Fraser says, 'Afternoon boys.'

White powder is visible on the tip of his nose. Angus has noticed it. He nudges me, taps his own nose, and says, 'Ching.'

Simeon says, 'I'll go get everything.'

He scampers off. It will appear suspicious if I ask him to bring salt, assuming there is any. Cheikh and Angus are conversing. Kiro is standing several metres away with his arms folded. He yawns again. Having wiped the tip of his nose, Fraser shifts his weight from one foot to the other. He says, 'Hey, Cheikh, what's up?'

'Everything is good, thank you.'

'Pleased to hear it, buddy.'

What is required is what is termed camaraderie. It should enable Kiro to relax. A topic for communal conversation could facilitate camaraderie. Um ... Health and safety regulations. Simeon scampers in. He is clutching a packet of custard cream biscuits and a stack of Styrofoam cups. Fraser asks, 'Simeon, where are the glasses?'

'They're being washed offsite.'

'So, we're drinking Burgundy out of Styrofoam cups.' Fraser spins to face me. 'Jesus Christ!'

'Bevvie, bevvie, bevvie,' chants Angus. 'Let's get blotto.'

A corkscrew emerges from Simeon's pocket. As Fraser unscrews a cork, he says, 'Should really be left to breathe. But as we're already going to be committing one faux pas, fuck it!'

Kiro is still ignoring everyone. I say, 'Kiro, come and join the party.'

He mutters something inaudible and stomps over. Simeon pours the wine into cups. Kiro snatches a cup and gulps from it. Everyone is drinking wine except Simeon who is guzzling orange squash. He is teetotal. This means more wine for everyone else. I pick up an open packet of custard creams, hold them out to Kiro, and say, 'Can I interest you in a custard cream?'

He looks at them, grimaces, and says, 'What are they?'

'Custard creams. This variety of biscuit is a staple of the funeral industry.'

'What?'

'Staple means a main or significant element.'

Kiro shakes his head. Following a gulp of Burgundy, he moves away from me. He better have that tattoo. Otherwise, I will fire him. Angus is jabbering to Fraser and Cheikh. Simeon is pecking at a custard cream. I watch Kiro crumpling his now empty cup. There is a risk he could leave. Matters need to be progressed quickly. Time for that health and safety conversation.

'Team members, a new bin bag regulation is about to be brought in.'

'Numpties,' says Angus.

'Not another one,' says Fraser. 'Nightmare these regulations. You should try working in a morgue. Walking on eggshells th—'

'I am talking to my team, Fraser.'

'Oh, sorry, Dyson, don't want to ruin your team party. I could always piss off with my Burgundy.'

Don't do that. I watch Kiro drop the fragments of his crushed cup on a table. Fraser opens a bottle of Burgundy and pours some into his cup. Meanwhile Simeon, his mouth full of custard cream, divulges further information about the new cremator. I say, 'Bin bags it is proposed, are not to be left unattended in public areas, in the event someone puts their head in one and suffocates themselves.'

'Numpties,' says Angus.

Cheikh expels air from his mouth and Kiro chuckles. This is more like it. I say, 'Health and safety regulations are becoming more ludicrous by the day.' Here goes. 'More wine anyone?'

'Aye.' Angus raises his cup. 'Fill her up.'

I pick up the bottle Fraser opened with my right hand and pour some into Angus's cup. I then say, 'Cheikh, more wine?'

'*Non, merci.*'

'Kiro?'

'Give me.'

'Find yourself a new cup then.'

Kiro grabs a Styrofoam cup with his right hand from the stack, marches over to me, and extends his right arm. I pretend to stumble forward and throw a substantial amount of Burgundy over Kiro's left arm. Emerald eyes fix on me. He crushes the cup, and spits, '*Jebi se! (Fuck you!)*'

'Dyson's blootered!' blurts Angus.

'Simeon, get some salt and water. Hurry.'

'There's no salt.'

Kiro lurches away. Where is he going? I set off after him. Fraser grips my forearm, and says, 'I'd leave him Dyson if I were you, he looks ready to batter you.'

I pull my arm free and hurry through the hall. As Kiro disappears into the men's toilets, I see him pulling off his top. I take my Nokia mobile phone from the side pocket of my suit jacket. Outside the door to the toilets, I count to five then push the door slightly ajar. Kiro is standing with his back to me at the sink. He is wearing only a vest. On the underside of his left forearm, I can make out a tattoo depicting a crown, beneath which are two eagles facing opposite directions. *Bingo!* While taking a photograph of him with my Nokia mobile phone, I cough to conceal the clicking noise. He spins around; I lower the mobile phone.

'What are you doing?'

'Come to check on the stain.' His left forearm is pressed tightly to his side. 'Well, is it coming out?'

'Two seconds it has been. What do you think?' He is glaring at my mobile phone, which is clasped at my waist. 'Why you have that?'

'Are you referring to my mobile phone?'

'Yes.'

'I was about to text someone; that's why I am holding it.'

'Leave!'

'Alright, I will.'

'Go!'

I depart and return to the hall. If that alleged genocidal maniac did not hold the promise of a hefty reward, I would fire him this instant for insubordination.

SEVEN

HE FOLLOWING MONDAY – 08:37 – I am jogging along Newton High Street. My destination is the Somali internet café. Immediately after the cremator christening-cum-team-get-together last Tuesday, I went to an internet café and emailed the Croatian vigilante organisation who are offering the reward. I used an internet café because I do not want them tracing the IP address to me. The email was sent from an account that I have, which is not registered in my name. Ever meticulous, I was careful not to divulge any details other than to say that he is in the London area, and that I am in contact with him. The photograph was also emailed. Whilst the tattoo was not visible in its entirety, the crown, eagles' heads, and the tops of their wings were discernible.

When I checked the email account last night, they still hadn't responded. Despite the temptation, I considered it would be ill-advised to check the account from my desktop at home, in case their email contained a tracking cookie which activated on being opened. *The email will have arrived. I will claim the reward.*

When I burst through the café's door, the proprietor says, 'Back again.'

'Yes.' The place is crammed. 'Do you have any computers available?'

'In the far corner.'

I dash over to the computer. *Come on, be there …* 'Ahh!'

What a wretched start to the week. I set off at haste to work. A quick detour is made to Starbucks to purchase a caffè latte extra hot with soya milk.

It is 09:07, and I am in my floor's kitchen sipping coffee. A pair of council workers quit jabbering and leave the room. Through the window, I see a jogger in the plaza seven-storeys below. Pigeons scatter. They return the moment the jogger has passed and recommence pecking at the ground. A blob emerges in the plaza. Having filled my lungs, I hold my breath for three seconds before exhaling slowly. The blob grows larger; the pigeons take flight. I inhale through my nose, hold my breath, and gently pull my index finger. The recoil jolts my shoulder. The blob flops to the ground and the shot's echo resonates in the confined space. Blood and brains are oozing from the remnants of its imploded head. A woman screams. Passers-by hurry over. I close the window.

This is how events would have transpired were it not for the fact that I was holding a takeaway cup of caffè latte extra hot with soya milk, and not a high-powered rifle. I return to Burials and Cemeteries. Several minutes later Teleisha stomps over and grunts, 'Hi.'

'Good morning.'

Blob is a fitting term for the creature that has just collapsed onto what had, until the end of play on Friday, been Asma's chair. It has become even more blob-like in its absence. No doubt a result of spending the last six plus months ogling daytime television and wolfing fast food. If there were a god of heart disease, I would reconsider my atheist stance.

A mausoleum construction company have emailed their brochure. What their mausolea lack in stature, they compensate for with bad taste. One of the mausolea is pink. Pink is becoming increasingly associated with death. This is absurd, as there is no correlation between death and pink, other than maggots. If common decency prevailed, pink memorial structures would be made illegal. The mausoleum I am currently viewing is a Romanesque violation, complete with toga-clad sculptures of the deceased and Corinthian-style columns, astride of which are Essex cherubs. I will never permit my cemeteries to be defiled by these monstrosities.

Why have they been so slow in responding to me? It is most unprofessional of them. They better still be offering that reward. In the passageway that runs past my desk, Frank and Terrence of the failed hair transplant, are discussing England's forthcoming cricket tour of India. Throughout the remainder of the morning, I work fastidiously. Two minutes before midday, I hear chewing. Opposite me, Teleisha is slouched at her desk devouring a doughnut.

'Eating is not permitted in Burials and Cemeteries.'

It groans, hauls itself up and waddles off in the direction of the kitchen. I put on my suit jacket and go to the Somali internet café. *Come on, be there.* Every computer is occupied. I wait twelve minutes for one to become available. While the email inbox loads, I drum my fingers against my thighs.

··

Mon, Nov 15, 2008 at 10:59 AM, <upiti@pravda.hr> wrote:

Dear Ignotus,

We welcome your investigation. You now progress to step two.
Provide us DNA proof of subject. Hair Sample/Saliva.
Send to P.O. Box 148, HR-1000 Zagreb, Croatia.
DO NOT write PRAVDA anywhere on package.

Be careful, subject is genocidal. Remember this is for
Justice. We trust in you to receive award.

To Justice and Beyond,

PRAVDA

....

'YES!'

People are looking at me. The establishment's owner comes
over and says, 'You seem happy, sir. Did you win lottery?'

'No, but I know what the numbers are going to be.'

'You want to share with us?'

'Certainly not.' I stand up. 'However, I am prepared to buy a
Somali coffee for everyone in here.'

'Everyone?'

'Yes, everyone.'

He leans into me and whispers, 'It would be inappropriate
for you, a man, to buy drinks for the Muslim women here.'

'Well, in that case just the men.'

'As you wish.'

When he announces my offer, there is cheering and clap-
ping. Having paid for eight coffees, I depart.

*

That evening – Eva is perched on my sofa watching television
and nibbling on her fingernail. I sit down on the other end of
the sofa to her and have a sip of chardonnay. She says, 'Can I
have some more wine?'

'I filled your glass five minutes ago.'

'Well, I've finished it.'

'You drunk that fast.'

'I need something to take my mind off the other stuff.'

I go to the kitchen, get the bottle of chardonnay, and refill her glass.

'So, you have gone cold turkey?'

'Yes! It's stressing me out bigtime.' She pulls on a length of her hair. 'The medication the doctor prescribed me isn't doing much.'

'Surely you weren't that addicted to the cocaine you were buying off Blood Letz, or rather getting on tick.'

Eva shifts her position on the sofa so that she is facing me. She is pale and there are bags under her eyes. She says, 'It wasn't powder that was the problem, it was crack.'

'You've been smoking crack. No wonder you accrued so much debt.' I point at her. 'It's a loser's game.'

'I know that!' she blurts. 'Not totally addicted to it, just got a bit of a habit. I need some help getting off it.'

Eva resumes nibbling on her fingernail. His DNA will be retrieved from a drink receptacle. I will offer him a drink, and then collect the glass, can, or Styrofoam cup once he's done, and post it to Zagreb. Simple.

*

Two days later – I am looking at the brochure for the residential rehabilitation centre that I have booked for Eva to attend. The brochure's front cover is a picture of rehabilitated drug addicts running through lush grass. Their arms are outstretched and they are smiling inanely. The residential drug addiction treatment course I have booked is extortionate. However, funding it will not be an issue what with my impending one point five million Euro reward. By the time she gets out I will have disposed of her dealer, and all that will be left of him will be that stumpy dreadlock entwined with yellow, green and red cotton. The brochure mentions the word *love* repeatedly. I know all about love. It is a noun and a verb. My decision to assist Eva is duty of care, not love.

Teleisha is chewing on something. With any luck it is ricin or cyanide. It was late today. Flexitime stipulates that everyone is to be in the office by ten. It didn't stomp in until ten-fifteen. I am convinced that Sunita conjured Teleisha's return to Burials and Cemeteries to place pressure on my department, in an attempt to discredit me.

Rakesha totters over, drapes herself across my desk, and says, 'Hi Dyson, how are you?'

'Fine. And yourself?'

'I'm well.'

'Pleased to hear it.' She smiles faintly and twirls a lock of brown hair in her fingertip. 'Why're you looking at me like that?'

'Because you look good.'

'Thank you.' At the desk opposite me, I hear Teleisha tut. 'Um, let's have lunch together sometime.'

'Yes, let's do that.'

'Great. How about Friday?'

'Friday it is.'

'Perfect. What shall we have?'

'Will give it some thought.' I fix my gaze on her hazel eyes. 'I know what I want for dessert.'

Rakesha winks at me; Teleisha tuts again. When Rakesha totters off, I type up the updated cemetery regulation notices, which will be pinned to my cemetery's gates. On hearing faint singing, I sit up straight in my revolving office chair. The muffled crooner is familiar. Teleisha is wearing headphones. When I go behind its desk, I see the Celine Dion impersonator from *X Factor* on its computer screen.

'Turn that off.'

Yet another tut. I picture myself brandishing a hand-held electric cremulator high above its head. The device's whirring metal balls emit a sonorous sound as they bear down upon it. Fragments of flesh and bone fly in all directions. My office telephone is ringing.

'Good afternoon, Burials and Cemeteries.'

'Dyson!'

'Rebecca.'

'I'm at Newton New and I've got a serious problem.'

'Essex Cherubs?'

'Dyson, this is no joke.'

'What is the problem?'

'Kiro.' *Ahh!* 'Can't believe what he's done. Well, I can. He was messing around when I came to check up on them. Throwing rubbish at Angus like a big baby. Told him to stop. And you know what Kiro did?'

'What did he do?'

'Called me a lesbo and a dyke!' *This could be a big problem. The council considers homophobic insults to be tantamount to mass shootings of school children. If Sunita gets wind of it, my gold mine could be gone.* 'Dyson, are you there?'

'Yes.'

'What do you have to say?'

'Insubordination is not tolerated in my department. You can be rest-assured that I will be taking the appropriate disciplinary measures.'

'Pretentious drivel! You're hardly reassuring. What I'm doing here is reporting this sickening homophobic attack to you, the Head of Burials and Cemeteries. Your job is to pass it up the chain of command. That is correct protocol, right?'

'Calm down please.'

'Calm down?'

'Yes, I have this under control.'

'How?'

'I will be reprimanding him in person and cautioning him over his future conduct.'

'Oh my God! Have you heard yourself?'

'This issue is under control, as I have already informed you.'

'You will be passing it up the chain of command then?'

Absolutely not. Kiro will potentially be fired and will disappear.

'Answer me?'

'Yes.'

'Good. That neanderthal is a nightmare and I want him fired, ASAP.'

She hangs up. I punch my palm. His DNA must be collected forthwith. It is too late for today; my cemetery team are finishing in twenty minutes. Are they due in tomorrow?

*

That evening – Eva is on my sofa watching television and biting on her knuckle. When I switch off the television, she says, 'Why did you do that, I'm watching it?'

I pass her the brochure for the residential rehabilitation centre. Having gawked at the front cover, she flicks through the brochure. Her eyes are watery.

'I have paid for you to attend their residential drug rehabilitation treatment course at their headquarters in Kent.'

Eva drops the brochure on the sofa and throws her arms around my neck. Her cheeks are wet. She says, 'You do care. Thank you so much, this means everything to me. I love you.'

Her arms remain around my neck for quite some time. When she removes them, I sit down on the sofa. She perches on my lap and talks about her hopes for the future. I have spent my entire credit card limit on the rehabilitation centre and her outstanding energy bill. Further funds are also required for Blood Letz. He will of course be reimbursing me with his life. Whatever happens I will be claiming the reward for finding the errant Darko Draganović. Factors such as Rebecca will not prevent me from doing so.

'Dyson, is everything okay?'

'Yes, I'm fine.'

'You look stressed.'

*

As I descend headfirst into the toilet bowl, I am accosted by Beatrice's shrieking laughter. I awaken with my heartbeat reverberating in my chest. Eva clasps my forearm. Will it ever stop? It has been tormenting me my whole life. I lie on my back and look up at the ceiling. It even defiled my first memory. I was three years old or thereabouts. I was building a tower with toy bricks on my mother's kitchen floor, when it scampered into the room and kicked them over. I can hear it laughing now. *He, hehe, he* ... At seven a.m., I am roused by my alarm clock. I get up. Eva remains in bed. Having put on a lilac Forzieri tie, I review myself in my full-length mirror. What stares back at me is suave, sophisticated, and steadfast. Time to get moving.

I am ascending in the lift to floor seven when my Nokia *beeps*. It is Blood Letz demanding a further instalment on Eva's debt. I will visit the cashpoint later today. The lift door opens, and I disembark. Frank is conversing with Terrence. I bid them 'Good morning.'

They reciprocate. Frank follows me. He says, 'Busy today, but how about lunch at the Mandarin Tasty House tomorrow?'

'Evidently you are ready for some more reconstituted crab claws.'

'You know me too well, Dyson. Are you in?'

'Yes.' *No, I have a date with Rakesha.* 'Actually, I have an appointment tomorrow lunchtime. How about one day next week?'

'Next week it is. Catch you in a bit.'

My team started their shift at Boden Cemetery an hour ago. The plan is to get over there and collect the DNA. A drinks vessel will be employed for the purpose. I will purchase some soft drinks en route. There is an email in the inbox, informing me that the Bowyer's memorial bench is being delivered to Newton New later today. Yes, I remember the Bowyer's. The couple who died of food poisoning while on a package holiday in Turkey. And I remember their bench's design too. An abomination with a heart-shaped photograph of their beaming countenances integrated into its front. Alas, my waning cemetery is to be further defiled.

It is 10:02, and Teleisha still hasn't arrived. This is annoying. Burials and Cemeteries should not be left unoccupied during office hours. This is especially important at this time of day when the telephone tends to ring constantly, as it is doing currently.

'Good morning, Burials and Cemeteries.'

'My husband he die, a-hh, last night.' *And?* 'The family, a-hh, must do ceremony. You know good place for organise Hindu cremation ceremony?'

'*Mukhagni*. Indeed, I do. Your first port of call should be Indian Funeral Directors Ltd. They are located at thirty-three West Parade. They specialise in *mukhagni*.' I find their entry in the database. 'Here is their telephone number …'

A tremoring floor precedes its arrival. It dumps itself on its chair and stares across the desk at me with beady eyes submerged in a fat face.

'What?'

'You are late!'

'Nah, not really.'

'It was not a question.' A tut. 'I have been dealing with telephone calls that should have been dealt with by you. I am leaving. If there are any issues, telephone me on my mobile phone. Answer calls as they come in, respond to emails in the inbox, and make inroads with your in tray.' I stand up. 'Grammar.'

'You what?'

'Grammar is what I said. Pay particular attention to it in your emails and while talking on the telephone. Don't forget, you are representing Burials and Cemeteries.'

*

In Boden's memorial garden, a scruffily dressed woman is emptying a carrier bag of breadcrumbs onto the ground. They are pecked at frenetically by motley-coloured pigeons. What a nuisance Pigeon Lady is. I will be contacting pest control. The maintenance staff are stationed by the Crimean War memorial obelisk, raking leaves and picking up rubbish. Black refuse bags are tucked into the waistbands of their trousers. I am carrying a plastic bag containing three cans of Sunkist purchased on the way here. For an obvious reason I am wearing gloves. Angus stops frantically raking and raises his chin. He hurries over to me, calling out as he does so, 'Alright, Big Man?'

'I am good. And yourself?'

'Cannae complain.'

I pass him a can of Sunkist. Having eyed the can suspiciously, he opens it and gulps the contents at a furious pace. In between gulps, he says, 'You heard aboot Gers football club?'

'As in Glasgow Rangers?'

'Aye. Nae dosh. Oot the Champions League.'

'Well I never.'

Angus spins around and shouts, 'Oi midgie raker!'

After depositing a crisp packet in a bin liner, Cheikh trots over. Darko/Kiro continues raking.

'*Bonjour Monsieur Devereux.*'

'*Bonjour Cheikh. Ca va?*'

'*Ca va bien.*'

Cheikh takes off his right glove and shakes my gloved hand. I give him a can of Sunkist. He thanks me and returns to his duties. Angus joins him. I go over to Darko/Kiro, and say, 'Good morning.'

He shoves a wadge of leaves into the bin liner at his feet, and mumbles, 'Hey.'

'I have brought a drink for you.'

He smirks and says, 'To spill on me?'

'No.'

'Give me!' He seizes the can off me. It has a green X on its base, which I wrote with a marker pen. His emerald eyes fix on mine. 'What?'

'Nothing.'

He grunts and moves away from me. Through the corner of my eye, I watch The Genocidal One open the can of Sunkist and slurp from it. I wander off and inspect the graves that have been affected by subsidence. As I do so, I pretend to make notes in a notepad I brought for the purpose. Angus has finished his drink and is currently flattening the can with stamps of his foot. Cheikh stops raking and takes a sip from his can. Darko/Kiro has not drunk any more of his Sunkist. At this rate, I will be waiting all day for him to finish it.

Time passes. A butch figure is stomping up the path. It is Rebecca. Her intrusion is unwelcome. The plan was to avoid her this morning. She is approximately a dozen metres away when I call out, 'Morning Rebecca, sunny day isn't it?' No response is forthcoming. She continues stomping towards me. Having stopped an arm's length away, she stands facing me with her hands placed on her thick hips. She has dyed her spiky hair a lighter shade. 'Like the highlights.'

'Don't you candy-coat me! Give me an update on Kiro?' Her right index finger extends in my direction. 'Why's he still here? Shouldn't he be on suspension already while he's being investigated?'

'No!'

'Why not?'

'Firstly, Kiro is needed in my cemeteries, as you should be acutely aware.'

'Can't believe this.' She juts her chin at me. 'You've spoken to the senior people at the council, I take it?'

'Yes, I have discussed your issue with other senior staff at the council.'

'Sunita's aware of it?'

'Yes. We are currently deliberating on the best course of action.'

'Oh yeah.'

'Yes. I spoke to Dar, Kiro, when I arrived here. Presently, I am giving him the opportunity to digest the information I relayed. I was about to speak to him again when you poled up.'

'Don't let me stop you. Go on!'

'Very well.' I stroll over to Darko/Kiro. Rebecca is watching me. It is imperative that this aggressive and uncouth woman does not bypass me and go directly to Sunita, or my dinner ticket could be swiftly removed. My reward must be secured prior to this matter potentially escalating. 'Kiro.'

'What?' I position myself with my back to Rebecca and adopt what she will discern to be a confrontational stance. My hands are placed on my hips, in the same manner she employed when confronting me so rudely. 'What, I said?'

'You've done a great job here with the leaves and rubbish. Boden has never looked so tidy. As is the case with my other cemeteries.'

'What do you want?'

'Rebecca has taken offence at remarks you allegedly made regarding her sexual proclivities.'

'Proclivities,' he spits.

'Yes, proclivities. Proclivity is a tendency or inclination towards a particular activity.'

'Lezza!'

'Indeed, your observation is correct. However, please note

that derogatory comments, or near on any comment for that matter that cannot be classified as praise, are ill-advised when that comment is related, or directed at a person concerning their appearance, ethnicity, religious inclination, or sexual practices. In future, refrain from commenting on any of those subjects during working hours. Thank you.'

Kiro chuckles. He says, 'Pompous is the word you English use for people like you.'

I clench my fists. If these were not exceptional circumstances this insubordination would not be tolerated. Insulting the Head of Burials and Cemeteries is no minor infraction. I enquire, 'How is the Sunkist?'

'First time I try Sunkist. Like Fanta, but shitter.'

He picks the can up off the ground, raises it to his mouth and throws his head back. The can is plonked at the foot of the obelisk.

'Have you finished your drink?'

'Yes!'

He resumes raking. I pick up the can and deposit it in my carrier bag.

'I will put your can in the recycling bin.'

'Whatever.'

Rebecca is still watching me. As I walk off, I say, 'Goodbye Kiro, keep up the good work.'

The words are augmented by me throwing my left arm up. This will give her the impression that I am rebuking him. Rebecca approaches me and says, 'So, what did he have to say for himself?'

'Not a great deal, I did most of the talking. He has been told in no uncertain terms that his behaviour was unacceptable. Kiro was apologetic.'

'Yeah, right.'

'He has learnt his lesson. Goodbye. Enjoy the rest of your day.'

Rebecca ejects air forcefully from her nostrils. The Genocidal One has stopped raking and is watching me. It will appear suspicious if I do not collect the other Sunkist cans. I go over to Cheikh, and say in French, 'Keep up the good work. I will drop your can in recycling on the way out.' He thanks me and passes me his empty can. Kiro/Darko is still watching me, as is Rebecca. 'Angus, give me your empty can, I will put it in the recycling bin on the way out.'

'I do, Big Man. Nae bother.'

'Give it to me.'

After dumping Cheikh and Angus' cans in the recycling bin, I set off at a brisk pace for the post office.

EIGHT

IT IS FRIDAY LUNCHTIME, and me and Rakesha are dining at an Asian-themed eatery in the mall. It could best be described as Mandarin Tasty House meets salad bar. There are fish tanks on the walls and light orchestral-style music fused with the sound of running water. Rakesha nibbles on a vegetable spring roll, which is clasped delicately between chopsticks. I pick up a length of black seaweed from my plate and examine it. Whilst the Orient-inspired salad I ordered is undoubtedly infinitely healthier than Mandarin Tasty House fare, it is no more appetising.

'Dyson, I'm surprised such a dashing man as yourself hasn't been snapped up by somebody already.' She winks at me. 'Most of the desirable men out there are married and settled down. But not you. How come?'

I fix my gaze on her when I reply, 'I have exceptionally high standards.'

She resumes nibbling on her vegetable spring roll. I insert a sliver of sesame oil-drenched carrot into my mouth. Utterly tasteless. I will not be returning here.

'So, you don't have any children then?'

'No, I don't.'

'Got my daughter Shaneeka as you know.' She looks at me. 'Work and her don't take up all my time though.' She smiles. 'If you'd like to do something sometime with me, that'd be good.'

'Count me in. We will do something soon.'

I am in the process of raising a piece of seaweed to my mouth when my mobile phone *beeps*. It is a text message from Blood Letz demanding a further instalment on Eva's debt. What with everything else going on, I have not got around to making a further payment.

'This text message is work-related. I will quickly reply to it.'

'Please do. No rush.'

I inform Blood Letz that I will furnish him with a further two-hundred-and-fifty pounds at the skateboard ramp in forty minutes' time. Rakesha asks me about my work and what I like doing in my free time. I have finished the Orient-inspired salad and am currently deliberating over whether to risk ordering a dessert. Most of the dessert menu consists of uninspiring fruit-based offerings. However, there is green tea sorbet. Rakesha sidles in her chair over to me. While curling a length of brown curly hair in her fingertip, she says, 'Really enjoyed coming here with you and getting to know you a bit better. You're different to everyone else at the council. I like that about you.'

She purses her lips and slowly edges her face towards mine. Our lips are poised to touch, when I see out of the corner of my eye, Darren emerge from the Foot Locker store on the other side of the mall. Rakesha pulls away, frowns, and says, 'What is it?'

'Darren.'

'Oh God!'

He strolls into the restaurant and swaggers over to our table.

'Thought it was you two. You alright?' Darren pulls a shoe box from his Foot Locker bag. 'Check these wicked trainers aht!'

Rakesha sighs and calls to the waiter, 'Bill please.'

She insists on splitting it. Outside the restaurant, I say, 'Have an errand to do, so I will see you two in the office this afternoon.'

'Later,' says Darren. 'Alright luv, let's go.'
'Don't call me that.'

*

Blood Letz and his accomplice are loitering by the skateboard ramp. There is no sign of the girls or the mastiff. I approach them. Blood Letz says, 'Yo, where you been bitch?'

'Excuse me?'

'Deaf or something? Said where you been? Ain't paid shit. Two hundred 'n sixty is all. This is no game. Cough it up!'

'Here is two-hundred-and-fifty pounds.' I extract the money from my wallet. He snatches the wad and counts the notes. 'It's all there.'

'I be the judge of that, fool.' He is grinning at me. 'Wearing posh threads but can only pay peanuts. How's dat?'

'I have a temporary cashflow issue.'

'Get a better job. Sell shit, be a rent boy.'

The pair laugh hysterically.

'Goodbye.'

I walk off. Blood Letz will not be so haughty once it's been disembowelled and beheaded.

'Didn't say leave.' I keep walking. 'Will be texting yah. 'N don't be ignoring me, or I'll fuck you up 'n your bitch, you get me?'

I grip the inside lining of my trouser pockets to prevent myself grabbing an object off the ground and commencing an assault upon its person. It will certainly get me when I execute it. The cotton-entwined dreadlock at the front of its head will be transferred to my fly-fishing tin, where it will remain for perpetuity. I am in the process of turning onto the street when I see that it and its accomplice are moving off in the opposite direction to me. Where are they going? Perhaps their destination will be of interest. However, what with my extended lunchbreak I should be getting back to Burials and Cemeteries. My department is after all presently in the hands of the gorging, grammar grievance. But this is a good opportunity to potentially discover something about Eva's discourteous dealer.

The pair are up ahead, conducting a transaction with a youth on a BMX. When the pair lope off, I slink out from behind the railway arch and follow them, keeping a discreet distance. They cross a grassed area, bound up two flights of external stairs, go across a landing and disappear through a door halfway along it. The building they just entered has its name engrained on a plaque on its wall. Hope Court. I ascend the stairs to floor two. The flat they entered is number seventeen.

*

Death does not equal rest, as many incorrectly assume. Death is hectic. What with the countless freshly-hatched maggots munching on your corpse, rest is impossible. And even if you go for the cremation option as most do, the world doesn't just stop. The grass around your headstone needs cutting and the leaves raking. And if you are interred in one of the countless cemeteries like Newton New, there are empty cans of fortified cider and Tennent's Super that drunks will be chucking on top of you, after they've urinated on you.

Then there are the receptacles of gases, glues, solvents and aerosols, the school children sniff and then discard. And there are used condoms too. If I had a pound for every time a relative emailed me a photograph of their 'loved one's' gravestone, headstone, or Essex cherub with a condom encrusted to the stonework, I wouldn't be spending my days in the council.

It was last Thursday that I sent the Sunkist can by expedited airmail to Zagreb. It is now Wednesday morning. Conducting the tests may take a while, which is far from ideal what with the trouble my target has been causing. I have not heard anything more from Rebecca. With any luck her complaint can be brushed under the carpet, but I suspect this may not be the end of it.

I am inspecting the planner's drawings for a projected extension to Newton New's cremation area. My mobile phone is vibrating. It is Eva. I make my way through the office to the stairwell. En route, I tell Eva, 'One second please.' Having closed the door to the office, I say, 'Is this important? I am at work as you well know.'

'Dyson.'

'Yes.'

'I'm starting at the rehabilitation centre next week, and, um, I was wondering if we should have a send-off on the weekend. Maybe drinking and clubbing. Just the two of us, or another couple too if you can think of anyone.'

'Clubbing? Eva, you have a drugs dependency issue. Clubbing entails drugs, at least in your case.'

'Just a small blowout before I go in. A last hurrah. Not crack, I promise. That's what my problem is. Something else.'

'And I suppose you expect me to fund this escapade?'

'I'll make it worth your while.'

It appears that I will be procuring some of Blood Letz's finest. I will furnish him with a small instalment at the same time. It is a good thing that I am poised to claim a one point five million Euro reward, otherwise I would be feeling rather impoverished what this deluge of Eva-incurred expenses. No sooner have I returned to my desk than my office telephone rings.

'Good morning, Burials and Cemeteries.'

'Ashton and Sons' practices wouldn't be acceptable in an abattoir,' says Fraser. 'How they're still operating in the funeral business is beyond the pale. They're not even a member of the NAFD; can you believe that?'

'Yes.'

'Yes? Do you even know who I'm talking about?'

'Ashton and Sons are located by the intersection, near the Somali internet café.'

'That's them, yeah. Animals.'

As Teleisha has stomped off somewhere, I ask Fraser a non-work-related question.

'Fraser.'

'Shit, nearly run out of arterial conditioner. Yeah?'

'This Friday, me and Eva are having drinks followed by clubbing. In the highly unlikely event that you're able to persuade a female to join you, you are hereby invited.'

'Thanks, count me in. Have just the girl in mind.'

'I trust she has a pulse.'

I hang up.

On the other side of the partition that separates Burials and Cemeteries from sport, leisure and culture, a group conversation is underway. I can hear Rakesha and Grace. There is also a Darth Vader-esque voice, which belongs to education's number two. Doyle had his larynx removed last year and speaks through a mechanical one. Grace says, 'Here's a photo of our new puppy.'

'*Ah*,' says Rakesha. 'It's cute. Would love to have a puppy like that.'

'That is so sweet, *zzzz*. Is it a, *zzz*, labrador?'

It is midday. At twelve-thirty I am braving the Mandarin Tasty House. Prior to that, I will pay a visit to the social services department. The social services database is a hive of information. It might contain something revealing about the property in Hope Court. Both days this week I have ventured down to floor four, where the department is located. On Monday I went during lunchtime, but most of the team were there and it was not possible to use one of their computers. Yesterday I was very busy. When I finally got a chance to visit social services, it was almost three o'clock and the entire team was in a meeting. With any luck today's visit will be more fruitful. All I require is the use of one of their computers for a minute or two.

Frustratingly, I discover that all the desks bar two are occupied. Another attempt will be made post-Mandarin Tasty House.

*

Four of us are lunching here. Myself, Darren, Frank, and housing's Elisa. I am currently chewing on a mouthful of Singapore fried noodles. Frank has a gulp from his bottle of Tsing Tao beer. Darren prods at a reconstituted crab claw on his plate, and says to Elisa, 'Have a bite on that.' She gapes at his plate. 'Go on, tuck in!'

She pierces the crab claw with a chopstick, raises it to her mouth, and takes a bite. She spits the contents into a napkin.

'Rank!'

How unladylike. Darren laughs and Frank peers up at the ceiling. Once they match the DNA which they surely will, what will be the next step? Claiming the reward might entail pointing the target out to an agent in a car with tinted windows, parked at the entrance to Newton New. Elisa says, 'Dyson, you look serious and you're not saying anything. Are you okay?'

'I am fine.' She ruffles my hair. 'Don't touch me!'

'Alright, keep your hair on.'

'Fuckin' *'ell*,' says Darren. 'Touchy Dyson.'

'She is the one being touchy, not me.'

Frank plonks his bottle of Tsing Tao on the table, and says, 'No need to bite her head off, Dyson. Elisa was just being friendly and concerned.'

Elisa says, '*Yeah.*'

I eat my Singapore fried noodles. Meanwhile, Elisa fiddles with her mobile phone and Frank and Darren talk about football.

*

13:23 – Most of the social services department are presumably on their lunchbreak. The only people here are two female staff members, who are chatting to each other at their desks on the other side of a partition from where I am standing. They haven't noticed me. I crouch down, slide onto a chair and tap the *Enter* key on the keyboard in front of me. Whoever's computer this is has unfortunately logged off. The women are still chatting. No one is looking this way. Having shifted across to the neighbouring desk, I tap keys on the keyboard. I'm in. The database is open. A man is trotting along the passageway that runs beside social services. I swivel in the chair, so my back is turned to him.

I type 17 Hope Court into the database and press *Enter*. The name Pegasus Kallon appears. His date of birth is listed as 12/10/1985. Blood Letz must have been born around then. He could be Pegasus Kallon. There are tabs at the top of the page. One of the tabs is labelled *Details*. I click on it. There are some notes. I read them. Mr Kallon is the sole occupier of the property. He has been living there since 2006. I drum my fingers on the desk. Kallon is a common Sierra Leonean surname. When Blood Letz took the furniture from Eva that day, he revealed the stock of his handgun. It was engraved with the colours of the Sierra Leone flag. Green, white and blue.

Meagre Martin is coming this way. I slide off the chair and move away from social services.

'Long way from your department, mate.'

'Was visiting some people down here.'

'Hah, remember that chat we had about the funeral songs?'

*

It is now 18:39, and I am in the Somali internet café. The vigilante organisation has not sent confirmation that the DNA sample arrived. However, I am aware from the tracking number I was issued that the parcel did arrive and was signed for. I am in the process of typing Pegasus Kallon plus Newton into *Google* when the establishment's proprietor approaches me.

'You are here again.'

'Indeed I am.'

'Can I get you something to eat or drink?'

I rotate my chair and inspect the sweets behind the plastic screen by the counter.

'Yes, I will have two Somali donuts, please.'

This internet café's insistence on serving desserts is the reason why the keyboards here are often sticky. While sticky keyboards are disagreeable, it is preferable that the stickiness is a result of sugar, and not porn consumption. Two Somali donuts on a saucer are deposited on the desk beside me, along with several paper serviettes.

The top result is an article from the local newspaper, *The Newton Post*. It is from September last year. The article is about ten Sierra Leonean child soldiers, who were granted asylum in the borough eight years ago during the country's civil war. One of the ten names listed is Pegasus Kallon. There is a picture of him sitting beside a floral-frocked social worker. This smirking ex-child soldier is Blood Letz. Excellent, I have his address. The article states that the child soldiers participation in the Sierra Leone Civil War had entailed witnessing the killing of civilians, rapes, forced amputations, and cannibalism. *They are all flourishing in Newton's warm multi-cultural embrace.* A spurious claim, even by newspaper standards. One of the ex-child soldiers is apparently training to become an accountant, another a doctor, a third a human rights lawyer.

The second listing on *Google* has the title 'Cash Converter Cannibal'. The term *Kallon* is missing. I read the article it links to. *A Newton pawn shop employee killed and ate the hearts of three borough residents.* I remember this. The refugee and ex-child soldier was found not guilty for reason of insanity. He is incarcerated in a psychiatric hospital. An associate of the cannibal, who gave his name as Pegasus, is quoted as having told the local media, *All of us ate human hearts in the war cos it gave us power.* It is doubtful that Blood Letz is capable of saying anything that coherent.

NINE

I HALF EXPECT the green laser lights penetrating the darkness to be followed by a volley of pops, then screaming, as partygoers' heads explode, splattering their fellow revellers with brains. Wailing partygoers clutch at gaping wounds as they clamber over bodies in their haste to reach the exit. But the shots never come. The crazed horde bounce about to the commercial techno being disgorged from the speakers. Eva's lithe body is swaying to the music. She is wearing a tight fitting armless mini dress with a transparent back. Eva pulls me by the arm through the throng of revellers to the bar. While shaking her empty Smirnoff Ice bottle, she says, 'Want another. Imagine this time next week I'll be on courgette smoothies ...' Eva orders herself a Smirnoff Ice and a rum and coke for me. She slips something into my trouser pocket, and whispers in my ear, 'It's really nice.'

I weave through the horde to the toilets. Having locked myself in a cubicle, I perch on the toilet seat and inspect the self-seal transparent bag Eva passed to me. It has Pegasus' trademark green skull printed on it. I visited Pegasus, or Blood Letz as he likes to be known, after work today. *Kidding me fool,* he said. *Owe me dough 'n you're here to score shit. Full-on fuck-up you are!* As well as purchasing some of his finest, I gave him a hundred pounds towards Eva's debt. I crush the cocaine between my travel and library cards then roll up a twenty-pound note.

When I return to the bar, I find Eva with Fraser and an Oriental girl. Her long, blonde-tinted silky hair hangs to the small of her back. Her petite frame is clad in a mini skirt, silk top and stilettos. Presumably her presence is a result of an outstanding funeral debt.

'Dyson,' says Eva. 'Look who's here.'

'Yo!' says a suited, bleary-eyed Fraser. He is holding an open bottle of champagne. 'What's up?'

'Good evening.'

'Dyson, this is Kei.'

'Hello Kei.'

She clasps my hand in her immaculately manicured fingers, and says, 'Hi, nice to meet you, Dyson.'

While Eva and Kei converse, I sip rum and coke. Fraser is scuttling from side to side in crab-like fashion. Following a lengthy swig from the champagne bottle, he screams, 'Party time!' He presses the champagne bottle into Kei, barges me with his shoulder, and says, 'Please excuse me, just going to powder my nose.'

Eva and Kei grab me by the arms and drag me to the dance floor. The two of them shimmy into each other and giggle. Kei takes a gulp from the bottle of champagne then passes it to Eva. I opt for a combination of rotating movements with both wrists and a twisting motion with my body. The girls are laughing. Kei points at me with a purple-tinted talon, and shrieks, 'That is pathetic.'

I grit my teeth. Having analysed revellers dance routines, the decision is made to discard the wrist rotations, in favour of pumping my arms and moving my feet. This is easy, I am successfully masquerading as a clubber. Eva raises her thumb and Kei nods at me. As I dance, I continue to innovate my routine, incorporating elements of the better-received efforts of those around me.

Fraser stumbles over and bellows, 'PARTY!'

He spurts a jet of champagne up into the air. When it showers him, he laughs hysterically. A reveller wipes champagne off his sleeve, and shouts, 'Dude, what's the matter with you?'

A girl paws her champagne-spattered shoulder, and shrieks, 'Grow up, Grandpa!'

Fraser shoves his bottle of champagne at Kei and lurches off in the direction of the toilets, making peculiar train-like motions with his arms as he goes. Me and the girls wander over to the bar area. Eva says, 'Fraser's off his face.'

'Yeah,' says Kei. 'At least he's buying us champagne though.'

I insufflate a second line of cocaine in the toilets. Tonight is going well considering, and as long as Celine Dion has not made a foray into commercial techno, it should continue in the same vein. Back in the bar area, Fraser holds the tails of my shirt as if it were a sledge. I spin around. Strands of hair are plastered to his forehead.

'Stop touching me!'

We go to the dance floor. Fraser rubs his groin on Kei's silk-draped posterior. She slaps his wrist.

'You're gross!'

Fraser roars with laughter and gulps from his bottle of champagne. He glances at his watch.

'Jesus Christ, is that the time? The wife's going to kill me.' He passes me his champagne bottle. 'Got to fly. It was wild. Don't do anything I wouldn't do.'

He lurches off. Eva and Kei rub their bodies against each other and giggle shrilly.

*

An hour later – Eva and Kei are entwined in an embrace on the hotel's bed. Eva is wearing only black lace suspenders while Kei is naked except for her stilettos. I am sitting in a chair watching their frolics and sipping Pinot Noir. It is medium-bodied and has an aroma reminiscent of black cherries. I pick the bottle up and inspect the label. This Pinot Noir originates from France's Côte-d'Or region. The alcohol content is twelve point five percent. Eva looks up from Kei's nether regions and gapes at me.

'Oh my god, you're reading!'

Kei's mouth is hanging open. Eva bids me to come over with fluttering motions of her hand. I undress, fold my clothes, place them on the chair, and then move to the bed. Eva teases Kei's clitoris with the tip of her tongue and fingers her vagina. Kei writhes about and sucks on her right index finger. She removes her finger from her mouth, clutches onto my neck and bites on my lower lip. Eva rolls over and fastens her lips over my cock. Kei positions herself so that my face is next to her vagina. While Eva performs fellatio on me, I flick Kei's clitoris with my tongue.

Eva and Kei are wrapped in each other's arms, kissing. I pick up the bag of cocaine from the table beside the bed, pull down my foreskin and sprinkle powder on the head of my penis. After sliding on a condom, I re-join them. Eva sits up. Her mouth is smeared with lipstick and vaginal fluids. She empties powder onto the table, closes a nostril, and *snorts*. She then scoops up powder with a piece of paper and sidles over to Kei, who is kneeling on all fours. Eva blows the powder into her anus.

I am crouched on the bed, astride of the kneeling Kei. When I angle my cock into her anus, she emits a rasping moan. Having slid further into her, I commence thrusting in and out. Eva is lying on her back and Kei is licking her vagina. I coil my wrist around Kei's long, silky hair and increase the pace of thrusting. She moans, Eva bucks, and the bedframe bangs against the wall. On sensing the onset of my climax, I pull on Kei's hair, reach out with my left arm, insert two fingers into her mouth and stick them down her throat. She gags. The gag reflex causes her sphincter muscle to contract and tightly grip my cock. This is known as wolfing. When I extract myself from her, the condom is left dangling from her anus. Eva grabs my cock and gives it a tug. I ejaculate. As I peer at Eva's semen-splattered face, I ask myself, *Could this be love?*

*

08:33 – The following Tuesday – I have taken this morning off work, in order to escort Eva to the rehabilitation centre. She is due there at ten-thirty. We will be taking the train. The Somali internet café is remarkably quiet for this hour of the morning. I select a computer terminal in the corner. There is an email in my inbox from the vigilante organisation. They must have the results. I open the email.

....

Tues, Nov 30, 2008 at 6:51 AM, <upiti@pravda.hr> wrote:

Dear Ignotus,

DNA MATCH
You progress to step three.
Today at 15:00 GMT — (Telephone: +385 43 1 472 555)
Say password when phone is answered.
Password: odmazda4
DO NOT REPLY TO THIS EMAIL.
Be careful, subject is genocidal. Remember this is for
Justice. We trust in you to receive award.

To Justice and Beyond,

PRAVDA

....

What is step three going to entail?

A park – Kent – Me and Eva are sitting on a bench overlooking a pond, containing the usual array of water birds – Canada geese, mallards, coots, moorhens. There are also some exotic species, including several Mandarin ducks and a pair of Egyptian geese. Eva is biting her fingernails; a habit I deplore. With any luck, rehab will rid her of this recent repugnant vice, along with her fondness for crack cocaine.

'I'm nervous. Not sure what to expect in there.'

'It will be fine. They will keep you busy.'

'When I get out, I really hope I'll be more on top of things.' She grips my elbow. 'My ex-dealer being in the neighbourhood is going to be a challenge. I'll just have to stay away from him.'

'He may well disappear.'

'Why?'

'He might move on to pastures new, or something else could occur. His career choice is precarious after all. Any number of things could happen to him.'

Eva kisses me on the cheek, and says, 'Thank you for paying off some of my debt. It's been a godsend. I'll never get in this sort of mess again, I promise.'

She lights a joint. While she smokes, I look at the pond. When she has finished, we go to the rehabilitation centre. I carry her sports bag and she drags her wheeled-suitcase. The centre's garden is visible through the security gate's bars. Its lush grass is identical to the picture on the brochure's front cover, only there are no rehabilitated drug addicts running through it. Presumably they are locked inside receiving treatment. Eva is breathing heavily. She says, 'Thank you for organising this. I love you.'

I press the button on the intercom.

*

14:47 – Plastered on the walls of the Health and Safety educational facility, are signs that read *Do Not Run* and *Get Your Heart Checked*. Darren and several of his colleagues from bins are also attending this afternoon's training session. I take a sip of my caffè latte extra hot with soya milk. Darren is wearing his new trainers with grey, formal trousers. The instructor says, 'Let us go through the correct way to move a wheelie bin.'

Darren nudges me, and says, 'Fuckin' bollocks this.'

'That it is.'

In the chair in front of him, Imbecilic Irene twists around, and says, 'Darren, told you twice already, be quiet. Concentrate, it's important.'

What this is, is ludicrous. I am here because my cemetery maintenance team deal with rubbish. While the presenter talks, Imbecilic Irene makes copious notes in a notepad. It is two minutes to three. When this tripe concludes, I will telephone the vigilante organisation. The presenter continues droning on. My once proud nation's future is threatened by the bureaucratic nightmare that is health and safety regulations. Millions of working hours are lost each year at pointless training sessions. Sport is deemed so dangerous that schools are becoming too nervous to allow their charges to exercise. Successive governments have created a nation of morbidly obese hypochondriacs, who are threatening to drown the National Health System and the death industry in a sea of liquid yellow butterfat. Illness and Danger would be a more befitting name for such an erroneous organisation. Surging superpower China is not wasting their workers time on this nonsense.

'Thank you all for coming. I hope you found the session useful.' *Finally, it's over.* 'Does anyone have any questions?' Imbecilic Irene raises her arm. *Ahh!* 'Yes?'

'Please would you go through one more time the correct way to move a wheelie bin?'

I grit my teeth. Groans are audible. Darren leans into me, and whispers, 'Twat!'

'Approach the bin straight on and grip the handle with both hands, which must be shoulder-width apart ... The wheelie bin is to be pushed, not pulled. Pulling exerts unnecessary force on the back muscles ...'

The moment the session ends, I shoot off. Darren calls after me, 'Oi, wait up!'

I increase my pace. I am reluctant to make the call from my mobile phone, as I do not want to be traced, or for there to be any evidence that I have been in contact with the Croatian vigilante organisation. However, locating a telephone box is proving arduous. It seems that the telephone box is destined to go the way of the dodo.

Finally, a telephone box. I sprint over to it and dart inside. There is no dial tone. It takes ten minutes to find another telephone box, and this is Central London. Inside, a tramp-like specimen is quivering on the floor.

'Leave!'

No response is forthcoming. I drag it out by its heavily stained collar. The interior is immersed in the bitter stench of urine. I pinch my nostrils, insert a two-pound coin into the slot, and dial the telephone number which I have memorised. Zero, zero, three, eight, five ...

Bringg ... Bringg ... Bringg ... Bringg ... Answer Bringg ...

'*Halo.*'

I say 'Odmazda4,' as requested in their email.

'You told us in email you are in contact with the target,' says the woman at the other end of the line. 'Still the same?'

'Yes, I am in regular contact with him.'

'Friends, you two?'

'No, certainly not. He is my subordinate.'

'He answer to you?'

'Absolutely.'

'Good then. This means you can bring him to us.'

'I am not bringing him to Croatia if that's what you mean.'

'Of course. We will email you where.'

'This seems overly complicated. I could just point him out to you.'

'No! This not possible. We email further details. Goodbye.'

'Wait, what about the reward?'

'When you deliver target, you will receive reward in Euros.'

'Euros? And what am I supposed to do with all these Euros. Go to the bureau de change every two minutes?'

She hangs up.

TEN

TWO DAYS LATER – Why, when I work in Burials and Cemeteries, is everyone alive? Take this morning for instance. Council workers are mingling in the passageway, chattering inanely about television programmes, Christmas plans, family updates, and other banalities. On such a sunny, albeit cold day, I would rather be perched on a gravestone or bench in Newton Old or Boden, reading a newspaper and drinking a caffè latte extra hot with soya milk.

The incessant racket is not conducive to focusing on the sheltered housing proposal that Frank asked me to proofread. I place it on the desk, recline in my revolving office chair and feel the contours of the gold earring in my suit trouser pocket. It used to be worn by Frederick. He was a bi-polar sufferer and acquaintance of Eva's. Three years ago, I visited his flat to play chess. He took offence at an innocuous comment I made and attacked me with a knife, resulting in several lacerations to my arm. I turned the knife on him and drove it through his heart.

I am reminiscing about the event when Rakesha comes tottering along the passageway beside Burials and Cemeteries. She stops.

'Hi Dyson.'

'Good morning, Rakesha.'

'Haven't got a printer problem, just wanted to say hi.' She

tilts into me, and says in a quiet voice, 'Work is pretty boring today.'

'Would have said the same.' I meet her gaze. 'But it's looking up.'

'Ha, same for me.'

Having glanced to her right, she bends over, pecks me on the cheek and strokes her fingernails across my forearm. She totters off. Halfway down the passageway, she swivels her head and smiles at me. I wink. The vigilante organisation had still not emailed when I checked this morning. What do they expect me to do exactly? At lunchtime, I will go to the internet café. My mobile phone vibrates. It is a text message.

....

Today 10:37

Where u at bitch? ££££ ASAP or bang bang you get me? BL

....

Its disregard for appropriate etiquette presumably meant Blood Pegasus was never promoted in its child soldier unit and remained a private. Perhaps this is the reason it sought asylum here. It must be eradicated quickly, ideally prior to Eva leaving rehab. Its disappearance will be assumed to be gang related. The plan is to deal with it in the Hope Court address when no one else is in. From its desk, Teleisha calls out to me. Remarkably, its mouth is not full.

'Woman here on phone, asking why there aren't many pigeons in Boden Cemetery.' *Could social services rehouse Pigeon Lady in a padded cell somewhere. That pestering old bag is evidently utterly insane.* 'What do I say to her?'

'Tell her Boden's pigeons are migratory.'

My office telephone is ringing.

'Good morning, Burials and Cemeteries.'

'Yo Dyson.'

'Hello, Fraser.'

'Friday night was pretty wild. Kei's hot, isn't she?'

'That she is.'

'So's Eva. She looked gorgeous.'

'Yes, she did.'

'Did you three get up to any mischief?'

'What do you want?'

'Just phoning to say hi and to say if you fancy escaping from that public sector cauldron of yours, feel free drop in for tea. This afternoon is looking pretty quiet.'

*

12:11 – 'Sir, while you are waiting for computer, do you want some Somali donuts?'

'No.' They were stale last time. I inspect the array of sweets behind the plastic screen by the counter. 'A portion of Somali *halwa*, please.'

'Ah, you like our national dish, *halwa*?'

'Yes, hence why I ordered it.'

A computer terminal becomes available. The email has arrived.

....

Thurs, Dec 2, 2008 at 10:54 AM, <upiti@pravda.hr> wrote:

Dear Ignotus,

Thursday from 15:00 GMT (Tel +385 43 1 472 555)

Say password when phone is answered.
Password: odmazda5

To Justice and Beyond,

PRAVDA

....

I devour the *halva* and return to Burials and Cemeteries. The department's webpage requires updating with the latest PDF versions of my cemeteries' updated regulations. Asma was perfectly capable of converting the necessary files into PDFs and embedding them on the webpage. Teleisha is not. The photographs on the webpage could do with being updated too. I find two digital photographs of non-subsidence affected Boden graves. I resize them and alter the resolution.

*

15:11 – The plan is to make the telephone call and then wile away some time at Raven & Co. Funeral Directors. I have had quite enough of the council for one day. Telephone boxes were scarce in Central London, but here in the suburbs there are even fewer of them. As I walk past the Somali internet café, I contemplate making the call from in there, as they have booths for making and receiving international calls. However, they are far from private. I cross the junction. There is a telephone box. This is akin to catching a glimpse of an Amur leopard in the wild.

There is no tramp inside, the telephone works, and there is only a faint scent of urine. After several rings, the same woman from last time answers.

'*Halo.*'

'Odmazda five.'

'Listen, okay?'

'I am listening.'

'You in the London area too, yes?'

'Maybe.'

'I see from number.'

'Your point is?'

'You deliver subject to Southampton. It is not so far.'

'Is this a joke?'

'No. You have pen?'

'Yes, I have a pen.'

I extract a pen and a piece of paper from the inside pocket of my suit jacket.

'Write what I tell you.' *The sooner I claim the reward and am done with this draconian outfit the better.* 'There is a turning off the A335 north of Southampton, two kilometres from the airport.'

'Airport?'

'Yes, airport.'

'Preposterous. Considering that he is wanted overseas, airports must be as appealing to him as minefields are to normal people. He'll never agree to go to an airport.'

'You don't take him to airport. Two kilometres from airport I said. Road off the A335 take you to a business park. Its name, Kendle Business Park. You take him there. You must find an excuse for taking him there. Find a business at the business park, or invent a business that fits in with what you two do for work. He is your subordinate, you say on last call with me. Just say to the target you two have to work there, or do a delivery to there.'

'It would be far more convenient for all of us if I pointed him out to you here, and you picked him up and dealt with him yourselves.'

'No, I told you this already. We will deal with him there. We will be waiting for him. All you do is drive up and we take it from there. We will email you more details.'

'This plan of yours is not remotely convincing.'

'Before you sound confident guy. Now you say you are not capable of this?'

'I am capable of anything.'

'Okay. Friday afternoon is when it will happen. Await our email. Goodbye.'

'Wait a second.'

She hangs up. What an obstinate woman. This is going to take considerable planning. I exit the telephone box and make my way to Raven & Co. Funeral Directors. I ring on the doorbell. His secretary opens the door.

'Dyson, don't you look suave.'

'Yes. You're looking good too.'

'Oh, thank you. Come in. Fraser will be pleased to see you.'

I follow her through to the mortuary. There is an old woman on the slab. Fraser is pacing about and talking on his mobile phone.

'Yes Mother, I promise to speak to her today.' Fraser rotates his free hand through the air. 'I will speak to her about Matteo. I just told you that ... Goodbye Mother.' He hangs up. 'Hi Dyson.'

'Good afternoon.'

The secretary says, 'Is everything okay?'

'Ahh, family problem.' Fraser leans on the mortuary slab. 'My sister's Italian boyfriend.'

'How's that a problem?' says his secretary. 'Italians are handsome, romantic, cultured.'

'Matteo's not that type of Italian. He's the sort you come across in southern cities like Bari and Pescara, dragging an Alsatian around by a tattered piece of string.'

'Oh,' says his secretary.

Fraser says, 'Check this corpse out.' The secretary sighs and leaves the mortuary. I approach the slab. The elderly woman lying on it seems to be in a state of repose. 'Benign is the word I'd use for her.' Fraser passes me a photograph. 'That's Maureen on arrival.' She looks dehydrated and emaciated. 'Note the jaundice, the yellowing of the flesh.'

'How did you revive her?'

Fraser snatches a plastic bottle from a shelf, holds it out, and sings, '*Restoria*,' in operatic fashion. 'I added various humectants to the dehydrated and emaciated tissue to restore it and lend it a more natural appearance …' *There could well be something suitable in this mortuary to pacify Darko, if for whatever reason matters go awry on the trip to Southampton.* 'Exemplary work if I say so myself. Funeral is this evening. Then I'm flying up to Scotland first thing in the morning. Long golf weekend in Argyll of all things. Back Tuesday morning. Not sure if I mentioned it last weekend.'

His secretary enters the mortuary, and says, 'Your accountant is on the phone. Do you want to take it in here?'

'No, need to take a look at some spreadsheets. And I'll need you to find them.'

'Fine. Did you tell Dyson about our lunch at Mexicana Heaven today?'

Fraser picks up the bottle of Restoria with one hand and a bottle of humectant with the other. He shakes them with considerable vigour, as if they were maracas. At the same time, he emits what could best be described as Mexican festive noises.

'Fraser,' says his secretary. 'The accountant's on the phone.'

'So you said.' He returns the items to the shelf. 'Dyson, won't be more than ten minutes. We'll have tea when we're done. Want to come through or wait in here?'

'Wait in here.'

The pair leave. I survey the products on the mortuary's shelves. Dyes, humectants, make-up, Restoria, shampoos, boxes of tissues, plastic eye caps, disposable gloves. None of which are of any use for my purpose, though the gloves could come in useful for Pegasus, as I do not plan to leave fingerprints. There are syringes too, which could also come in useful for it, especially if filled with formaldehyde, of which there is plenty to be found here. Formaldehyde is what Health and Safety would describe as hazardous. However, my dinner ticket needs to be delivered alive.

There is an abundance of scalpels. I pick one up and watch the light reflect off its metallic surface. Darko would not be deterred or pacified with a scalpel. On the bottom shelf there is a bolt gun for bolting shut the jaws of the deceased. The instrument barely resembles a real gun, has only one shot, and unless fired directly into an orifice at point blank range, is hardly likely to endanger life.

This shelf contains water correctors, arterial conditioners and cavity chemicals. At the rear of the shelf are several identical bottles. I remove one of them. It has the word *chloroform* written on it. This former staple of the embalming industry must presumably still be used in the preparation of some embalming fluids, hence its presence here. The bottles of chloroform are too big to slip out unnoticed. I will return for them when Fraser is on his golf trip to Argyll.

*

11:07 – The next day – Frank approaches my desk.

'Morning, Dyson.'

'Good morning.'

'Few of us are having drinks after work today. You're welcome to join us.'

'I might come along for a quick pint.'

'Be one of the two pubs round the corner, I'm guessing. Hasn't been decided yet. Maybe see you later then.'

He wanders off. I will not be attending. Where was I ...? That was it. I was reading a letter of complaint from a borough resident, who lives adjacent to Newton New. Apparently, youths are running amok in there at night and making a considerable racket. Any youth breaking my cemetery regulations will be made to regret their transgression. The telephone on my desk is ringing. It is an internal number.

'Good morning, Burials and Cemeteries.'

'Dyson.'

'Sunita.'

'Come up to my office.'

'On my way.'

I cross my middle and index fingers. Having ascended to floor eight, I get two cappuccinos from the vending machine by the lifts. Sunita drinks this ghastly stuff. I don't. Choosing an identical drink is strategical. It may be required to curry favour. Copying habits and behaviours is an effective way of inveigling people. I am an expert on human behaviour. With a cappuccino clasped in each hand, I stroll over to the office and knock on its glass door with my forehead.

'Come in.'

'Good morning Sunita, I brought you a cappuccino.'

I place the cappuccino on its desk. It is glaring at me. This does not bode well. If there is an opportune moment for that *bindi* to tremor and the back of its head to explode, this is it.

'Sit down.'

Sunita is sporting overly large, silver hoop earrings.

'New earrings?'

'Sit down I said!'

I lower myself onto a chair on the opposite side of the desk to it.

'Rebecca just called.' *Ahh!* The red smear that serves as its mouth is curled downwards. 'Rebecca has been the victim of homophobic abuse.' *Not now. The timing is terrible.* There is

112

the sound of rustling paper. 'From a member of your cemetery team. A recent addition supplied by an agency.' It looks at a piece of paper on its desk. 'Kiro Burgan.' *Blame others, take no responsibility, minimise the damage.* 'Well?'

'This allegation is concerning.'

'If it is so concerning, why did you not inform me when you were made aware of it last week?'

'Because Rebecca did not tell me.'

It leans across the desk and says, 'Are you telling me Rebecca did not tell you that this Kiro character called her a lesbo and a dyke?'

'Precisely.' I sweep my hand through the air with the palm facing down. 'She did not.'

'What did she tell you?'

'Rebecca told me that she had concerns about Kiro. She said she suspected he was homophobic because some of his behaviour towards her had been inappropriate. However, she never told me he had insulted her sexual orientation directly. She did say though that he had been throwing litter at Angus and had been rude to her. I of course spoke to him in person about this and made it abundantly clear that we expect the highest standards of—'

'Enough!' Sunita flaps its henna-stained appendages. 'Rebecca isn't one to pull punches. She said she made it abundantly clear to you what happened and that you told her you would speak to me about it.'

'Rebecca is evidently confused.'

'Homophobic abuse is as serious as it gets. For whatever reason you have tried to brush it under the carpet.'

Another sweep of my palm is coordinated with, 'Absolutely not. I have been managing the situation. I have supported Rebecca and worked to resolve any cultural differences at Kiro's end. The aim being to create a more amenable working environ—'

'Be quiet!' A henna-stained finger extends towards me. 'You know the procedure full well. The initial complaint should have been reported to me, end of … This is what will be happening.' *Outrageous. This is my department's concern, not its.* 'Firstly, that man Kiro is out of here.' I clench my hands. 'The agency who supplied him have been told we don't want him here.' *Ahh!* 'They said they should be able to replace him fairly quickly.'

'This is unfair.'

'No, it's not.'

'The council purports to support cultural inclusion. So in that case, he must be given another chance. Kiro is from a different country, and therefore has a different set of cultural norms to here. My employee may have made a few faux pas. By making mistakes is how he learns. You don't even know exactly what occurred, whether he was even in the wrong.'

'Enough!' The henna-stained finger extends again. 'You haven't taken responsibility for this issue, and you have not followed correct protocol. What is confusing to me, is why you are protecting him? He is only a temp. He can be replaced in a heartbeat.'

'I am not protecting anyone. What I have been doing is managing the situation.'

'We're done.' It stands up. 'This isn't the end of the matter though. You have a lot of explaining to do. I will be discussing this with other senior members of staff, and we will decide what action is to be taken. Get back to work and don't make any more mess-ups. Go!'

I depart with my cappuccino, which did not prove advantageous after all. On the way downstairs, I smack the wall several times. This is so unfair, and the timing could not be worse. I must maintain contact with him. In Burials and Cemeteries, I telephone Rebecca.

Bzzt … Bzzt. Answer! Bzzt. Don't ignore me. Bzzt … Bzzt … Bzzt. Come on! Bzzt …

'Dyson, what the hell's going on over there? Sunita didn't know anything about my run-in with Kiro. Why is that? I told you explicitly I expected you to speak to her, and you agreed. That's the procedure in these kinds of situations.'

'There have been communication issues.'

'You what?'

'Communication issues is what I said.' Teleisha is watching me from its desk. 'The email I sent to her relating to your complaint got mislaid. It seems a junior staff member, who was meant to be dealing with the email, inadvertently deleted it, or filed it somewhere.'

'You're claiming you emailed Sunita about my complaint? Sounds like utter bollocks!'

'No, far from it.'

'Unbelievable. You're making it out this is her fault.'

Of course. 'Mistakes happen. No one is to blame. The important thing is that we learn and move on. Rebecca?'

'What?'

'I was wondering if you had a contact number for Kiro? If so, could you give it to me please.'

'What the hell do you want that for? He's been fired. He's not coming back. The council's done with him.'

'I am aware of that. However, it may be necessary for me to speak to him.'

'Why would it be necessary?'

'Regarding his less than satisfactory conduct here for starters. There is no number for him in our database.'

'Ask the agency who provided him then. They'll have his number. Don't bother me. Caused me enough headache already you have.'

'Do you have his number?'

'Jesus Christ! Wait a second … It's zero, seven, seven, two …'

After jotting it down, I say, 'I'll read it back to you.'

Rebecca has hung up. How ill-mannered. I have his telephone number at least. I am loath to contact him from a telephone associated with me. During my lunchbreak, I canter to the telephone box that I contacted the vigilante organisation from. The mobile phone rings, but no one answers. There is no option to leave a voicemail.

After work, I hurry to the telephone box and try the number again, but there is still no answer. Where is he? He cannot disappear on me. Those two women have put me in a stressful situation. I go to the gym next to my office. As a senior member of the council, I receive subsided membership. During my five-kilometre jog on the running machine, I visualise the forthcoming success of my mission. Visualising is a technique used by many high achieving people, including Olympic-level athletes. On alighting from the running machine, I see that there is a text message on my mobile phone from Eva's dealer, demanding an instalment on her debt. I will ignore him. My focus is solely on that one point five million Euro reward. *He will answer the phone. I will persuade him to come to Southampton. I will collect the reward.*

*

It is Monday morning, and I still haven't spoken to him. On the weekend, I made five attempts to reach him from a local payphone. The mobile phone rang, but he did not answer. *Where is he?* From Starbucks I purchase a caffè latte extra hot with soya milk. Perhaps, if I try from a different number he might answer. I set off at a trot for the Somali internet café.

I am inside one of the café's telephone booths. *Bzzzz, Bzzzz.* I run my palm through my hair. *Bzzzz, Bzzzz. Answer. Bzzzz, Bzzzz …*

'Who is this?'

'It's me.'

'Who me?'

'Me. The Head of Burials and Cemeteries.'

'What you want?'

'To help you.'

'Help, you. You no help. When you speak to me in cemetery, it seem no big deal my problem with the lezza. Now, I have no job.'

'It is a temporary measure.'

'Temporary? Some bitch she email the job agency.' *Sunita.* 'They angry. No job in future for me there. Maybe I leave from here. Move new place.'

'Don't do that!'

'Why not?'

'I will rectify the situation.'

'What does this mean rectify? You get my job back?'

'Yes.'

'Rubbish.'

'No, far from it. After all, I am the Head of the department. It is my decision to make.'

'This I do not believe. You crazy, pompous.'

'I am neither.' *How dare he.* 'I will have some work for you later in the week. Probably Friday. Keep it free.'

'How can I work if fired, hah?'

'The work is for my department, but it is offsite.'

'Offsite? Doing what?'

'Delivering.'

'Delivering?'

'Yes, delivering for the council. I will contact you on Thursday. Make sure you answer your phone.'

'Okay. Where you phone from? This number.'

'Possibly.'

'Possibly? Many calls I get from numbers I don't know on weekend and the Friday. From you these?'

'I tried you twice on Friday. The others were not me.'

'Okay. I do it.'

He hangs up. I punch the air. *Salvation!* I will inform him in due course that I require assistance with transferring Burials and Cemeteries 'stuff' to a sister department out of town. All I then have to do, is rent a van and fill it with convincing materials.

*

13:45 – I am leaning on a lamppost outside a charity shop, diagonally opposite Raven & Co. Funeral Directors. Through its window, I can see Fraser's secretary at her desk. I need to be alone in the mortuary, and it is likely that she will attempt to accompany me if not preoccupied. I watch her answer the telephone on her desk. This could be an opportune moment. However, she could bring the call to an abrupt end and join me in the mortuary.

Ten minutes later – A *sniffling* sound precedes a middle-aged couple shuffling past. They cross the road. Having dabbed handkerchiefs to their eyes, they press the funeral parlour's doorbell. The secretary lets them in. I wait for thirty seconds, then cross the road and ring the doorbell. The secretary totters over to the door, undoes the latch and opens the door fractionally.

'Hi, Dyson,' she whispers. 'Nice to see you. Um, Fraser's on holiday.'

'I left some papers in the mortuary last time I was here.'

'Oh.' She twists around and looks at the sniffling couple. 'Do you want to run in and get them?'

'Yes.'

I follow her through the office area to the mortuary door. After unlocking it, she totters over to the couple, and says, 'Sorry for the interruption.'

I go inside, close the door, take the folded-up papers I

brought with me from the inside pocket of my suit jacket, and place them on the vacant mortuary slab. Having slipped the empty gym bag off my shoulder, I approach the shelf containing the water correctors, arterial conditioners, and cavity chemicals. I reach to the back of the shelf, pick up two bottles of chloroform, and place them in the gym bag. The sniffling couple are still in here. As I walk through the office, I wave the papers.

ELEVEN

FRIDAY – I HAVE TAKEN the day off work. For today's trip, I will be wearing a light blue Ralph Lauren shirt. Blue is all about trust, loyalty and honesty. It radiates tranquillity and reduces stress. Lighten the shade, and the more relaxed and less confrontational the blue becomes. Understanding colour psychology is one of my many attributes. For trousers, I have gone with beige chinos. Beige combines well with blue. The pièce de résistance is a grey Nike baseball cap. It gives me a sporty look, perfect for the day's proposed activities. The cap also partially obscures my face, which could prove beneficial as I want to keep a low profile.

I enter the telephone box, drop a two-pound coin into the slot, and input the telephone number for the vigilante organisation, as instructed to do so when they emailed me yesterday. After several rings, the usual woman answers.

'*Halo.*'

'Odmazda five.'

'You ready to go?'

'Yes, I am ready.'

'He is ready?'

'Yes. I spoke to him yesterday. We are meeting at one o'clock.'

'Good. Listen. Coming into Southampton from north there

is a turning off the A335. It leads to business park. Kendle Business Park is its name.'

'I know, you said this the last time we spoke.'

'Between the A335 road and the business park there is a layby on the left. Half a kilometre from A335 precisely. It is by a wood. You cannot miss it. A red car will be parked there. Our people will be hidden in the trees, waiting. You drive into the layby and park. Tell him excuse like this. You have to telephone business park and tell them you arrive. Get out of your car. We take from there and give you reward. Five minutes we are done.'

'Very well.'

'From two-thirty we are ready.'

'I will deliver him then or shortly thereafter depending on traffic.'

'What car you come in?'

'A white transit van. Registration BX, zero, two ...'

'You have pen?'

'Yes.'

'Take this telephone number in case problem.'

'There won't be a problem at my end, I can assure you of that.'

No sooner have I left the telephone box than a text message arrives. It is from Eva.

....

Today 11:07

Hi Dyson,

It iz goin gr8, feelin good. Miss U loads. ☺

Eva xxxx

....

121

With Eva's imminent release, her dealer requires eradicating quickly. But before that it is time to conclude this Darko affair once and for all and claim what is rightfully mine. I am meeting him outside Boden Church in half an hour. Everything has been meticulously planned. The chloroform was tested on a neighbour's cat, which was lured into my flat with the promise of milk. A small amount administered on a cloth, rendered it unconscious for nearly a minute. On regaining consciousness, the cat teetered off to the balcony and promptly fell off. Compos mentis cats are agile and invariably land on their feet. Chloroformed cats less so. In the gym bag I am carrying, there is a change of clothes, the two bottles of chloroform, a large and relatively menacing serrated kitchen knife, some lengths of rope, cloths, and gags. If matters go awry, I will be able to pacify him.

The white transit van I rented is packed with three old kitchen chairs that I no longer want, an aged sofa someone discarded on the pavement outside my building, several cushions, a decrepit rug, and cardboard boxes. There are also piles of paper, bound with elastic bands. These are to be passed off as correspondence and documents. They have been diligently prepared for closer inspection. The top half a dozen or so pages are genuine Burials and Cemeteries-related paperwork taken from the filing cabinet at work, while the remainder consists of a combination of recycled paper and printing paper. I have also packed a large number of death business publications. *Morgue Monthly, Cemetery Restoration Quarterly, Embalming Enterprise,* and copies of the *Newton Cemeteries and Burials Newsletter.* This will all prove convincing should he wish to pry. I am currently applying the finishing touch – large Newton New Borough stickers to the sides of the vehicle. I found them in a stationery cupboard. *Voilà.*

I am parked in front of Boden Church, sipping a caffè latte extra hot with soya milk from Starbucks, which is more tepid than hot, despite it only having been purchased eight minutes ago. A bulky, hunched figure in a rain proofer appears in the rear-view mirror. It is not him. The time is 13:07. *Where is he?* There is a knock on the front passenger window. It is a traffic warden. I wind down the window.

'You can't park here!'

'I am meeting someone here.' I smile at her. 'Will be gone in a few minutes, I promise.'

'You have three minutes, I'm timing you.'

She wanders off. *Why isn't he here?* It starts pouring with rain. People hurry by with their hoods pulled up. Others are clasping umbrellas and holding shopping bags above their heads. There is another knock on the passenger window. A grim-faced, heavily built man, with close-cropped grey hair and piercing green eyes is squinting in. *Finally.* I wind down the window, and say, 'Good afternoon. It's very wet out there.'

He tugs on his purple anorak, and says, 'No problem, I have coat. Where are we going?'

'We are delivering the load in the back to a sister department out of town.'

'Where, I said?'

'Hampshire.'

'Hampshire big place. Where in Hampshire?'

'Near Southampton.' The parking attendant is coming this way. 'Get in, we must go.'

Following a grunt, he climbs in. I drive off. He says, 'A delivery of what?' He is studying me with his emerald eyes. 'Tell me?'

'Some furniture and a lot of paperwork.'

'Paperwork?'

'Yes, paperwork.' I roll my eyes upwards. 'The Data Protection Act means it can't be destroyed, and as there is no space to store it at the office, it is being transferred.'

'Pull over!'

'Excuse me?'

'Pull over I said.' Having clicked the left indicator, I draw to a halt at the side of the road. 'Show me these things.'

'Very well.'

He disembarks. I get out, unlock the van's side door and slide it open. He peers into the interior, then bounds inside. After lifting the rug and looking underneath, he runs a grimy thumb along a bundle of bound papers.

'Why you not bring other person to do this?'

'Angus and Cheikh are working in Newton New today and there is no one suitable in the office.'

'Okay. We go!'

He clambers into the front. I drive through the congested, rain-drenched suburban streets. In the rear-view mirror, I see a pair of eyes that are nearly identical to my own. Intelligent, resplendent, and lucid. Could the owner of these outstanding optical organs really be capable of the coarse behaviour he has been accused of?

This alleged war criminal is extremely large up close. He must weigh forty or so kilograms more than my lithely built self. While the chloroform has proven to be successful with cats, it may not be as effective on a gargantuan veteran of the Yugoslav Wars. The organisation best deliver on their promise and pacify him themselves. They are presumably planning on driving him to the neighbouring airport. The motorway is relatively quiet. At this rate of progress, I will arrive at approximately two-forty. The rain has ceased and shards of light are puncturing the grey gloom. He reaches forward, fiddles with the radio, and says, 'What music you listen to?'

'I listen to classical music primarily.'

'What classical music?'

'Tchaikovsky, Mozart, Chopin.'

'Chopin, hah?'

'Yes.'

'You know the music Chopin write for death. You say in English, *Funeral March*.'

'The finest piece of funeral music ever written.'

'Very fine it is, yes.'

Not only does he have exquisite eyes, but he also possesses an exemplary taste in music. He selects a classical music station, which is playing Mozart's *Piano Concerto Number Twenty-One*. I wonder if our shared taste in music extends to artists I despise.

'Kiro.'

'Yes.'

'Which artists do you hate?'

'You mean music artist?'

'Yes.'

'There are so many I hate. One particularly, hah, hah, hah!' The deep rumbling sound resonates through the vehicle. 'Two weeks ago, I was working in Newton New Cemetery. I was picking up rubbish near the funeral hall. A funeral was finishing at that moment. The guests were coming out of hall and a song also. Terrible song. Maybe the worst of all.'

'Which song was it?'

'*My Heart Will Go On*.'

'That festering sore of a song has been defiling funerals the length and breadth of my once proud nation. Listening to fingernails being dragged across a blackboard is preferable to being accosted by *My Heart Will Go On*.'

The alleged war criminal slams his massive fist on the dashboard, and spits, '*Jebi se*, Celine Dion!' *Jebi se* is evidently not a term of endearment. I tell him about the Quebec newspaper that named her Canine Dion, due to the frightful appearance of her pre-makeover teeth. He bellows with laughter and slaps his palms against his thighs. 'Hilarious! HAH! HAH!' When I observe him in the rear-view mirror, I see that the corners of his mouth are curled upwards and his features are creased with mirth. But his emerald eyes remain unchanged. 'You listen to Chopin, and you hate Dion. What other interests, hobbies you have?'

'My interests are diverse.' I click the right indicator and overtake the car in front. 'I am a voracious reader. Primarily non-fiction. I have a penchant for history.'

'Me too.'

'Really?'

'Yes. You read books about World War II?'

'I do indeed. I recently read *Stalingrad*.'

'Incredible book. I read it a few years ago.'

'A work of genius.'

The destination is twenty miles away. Johannes Brahms' *Violin Concerto* is playing on the radio. Having turned the volume down, Darko says, 'Problem at work with Rebecca is no big thing. Just a bit of banter, as you Brits say. Why I have to lose job for such a small thing?'

'I will resolve this matter very soon. You just need to be patient.'

'It is too late, must be. Maybe though you can speak to the job agency and say there is a misunderstanding. That I didn't do anything wrong and that it was, what you call, a miscommunication.'

'Certainly. I will telephone them once we have delivered this lot.'

'Good. That way they might find me new job.' He sighs. 'Rebecca cause big problem for me. It was nothing, just a joke. No sense of humour that *lezbača*.'

This trip is doubling as a Serbian language class. He turns the volume up on the radio. As we draw closer to the southern port of Southampton, the traffic increases. There is a sign for the airport. He is shifting his considerable bulk from side to side. This apparent anxiety could be due to the sign, or because Southampton is not much more than the breadth of the English

Channel away from the International Criminal Court in The Hague.

The turning is three miles from here. Heaving traffic results in me stopping directly adjacent to another sign for the airport. Steely emerald eyes are scrutinising me. Beethoven's *Moonlight Sonata* is playing on the radio.

'I take it, Kiro, you are familiar with Beethoven's *Moonlight Sonata*?'

'Yes, I know it.'

We are on the move. The turning is a little over a mile away. I drift over to the left lane and slow down. When I spin the wheel, Darko juts his chin at me, and says, 'Why are we going this way?'

'Because this is the way to the facility where everything is to be stored.'

'There is no council this way.' He prods a thick finger at the windscreen. 'This way business park.'

'Correct. Its name is Kendle Business Park. It contains a council-run premises, which is used primarily as a storage facility. Any more questions?'

He grunts and stares out of the window. There are woods on the left, as the operative said. I ease around a corner. The layby should be just up ahead, equidistant between the A335 and Kendle Business Park. There it is. The red car I was told would be here is not. However, there is a yellow car. Parked behind it is a Volvo estate police car. When I drive past, I see a policewoman peering through the driver-side window of the yellow car. This is not good. Darko is watching the layby in the side-view mirror. I continue driving. The business park is very close. I do not want to drive in there, as he will quickly realise that Kendle Business Park does not contain council premises. I will telephone the number I was given and make alternative arrangements. Perhaps the police car will drive off and the plan can still come to fruition. I park on the side of the road.

'Why we stop?'

'Because I am going to call my council contact.'

'For what?'

'To let them know we are in the vicinity and to enquire as to whether they are ready to take possession of our load.'

After unfastening my seatbelt, I remove the key from the ignition, and disembark. He is watching me. I close the door and stretch my arms up. Having wandered away from the van, I dial the telephone number the operative gave me. I keep one eye on the van. A man answers.

'Yes.'

I twist my head away from the van, and say, 'Odmazda five was the last password I was given.'

'You have him?'

'I do.'

'Where are you?'

'Have just driven past the layby. The police are there.'

'Yes, we had to leave. They are there for that yellow car. Must be stolen.'

'Quite possibly. You have a Plan B I assume?'

'When police go, we will come back.'

'That is not a Plan B. The police could be there for quite some time.' Out of the corner of my eye, I can see that he is watching me in the side-view mirror. 'Listen. He is apprehensive and suspicious. This matter needs to be resolved. Where are you?'

'We are at an airfield at the north end of airport.'

Darko has alighted from the van and is stomping this way. I twist my head towards him, and say, 'No problem, we will bring everything to the other location then.'

'What are you saying? Don't come here—'

I terminate the call.

'Kiro, change of plan.'

'What change?'

'They are insisting that we deliver our load to a different location, in the city itself.'

'Why they say this? It strange, yes?'

'To be expected. Things rarely run smoothly in the public sector. *C'est la vie*, it shouldn't take us too long to get there.'

He stomps over to the van and gets in. Once he realises that there is no other location, he may well flee. There is no way I am driving into the city. This matter needs to be resolved immediately. It is time to bring the chloroform into play. He is leaning out of the window.

'Hurry!'

My breathing is measured, and I am as calm and composed as when ordering a caffè latte extra hot with soya milk from Starbucks. I open the driver door and say, 'Can you check everything is secure in the rear? Something was rattling around in there. Possibly the sofa.'

'I heard nothing.'

'Please check.'

He grunts, grabs the key off me and exits the vehicle. When I hear him unlock the side door and bundle inside, I unzip the gym bag at my feet and take from it a bottle of chloroform and a cloth. I slip out of the van. Thudding footsteps are audible in the rear of the van.

'Everything okay, no problem here. We leave.'

'Check the chairs right at the back. It might have been them that were sliding around.'

Another grunt. When I poke my head through the side door, I see him squeeze past the sofa and step over several bundles of papers. Having unscrewed the top from the bottle, I hold the cloth to it, and turn the bottle upside down. I place the bottle under the van, jump in, and follow him. He is reaching for a chair when I pounce on his back. I wrap my legs around his waist, thrust one arm around his massive neck and force the cloth over his mouth and nose. He rams me into the side of the vehicle repeatedly. *Bang! Bang! Bang!* I grip resolutely on to him with my legs and keep the cloth clasped over his face. *Bang!* He makes a muffled 'P-p-p' noise through his mouth. He rams me again and pries my thumb off the cloth. I release my arm from around his neck, snatch the cloth and push it over his face. He lets go of my thumb and slams me into the side of the van. I press down on the cloth. Stars appear before me.

'P-p-p.'

He staggers out of the van with me attached to his back. A massive paw reaches behind him and grabs my hair.

'Ahh!'

'P-p-p.'

I keep the cloth pressed hard to his mouth and nose. This is nothing like the cat. He staggers across the ground with me fastened to him. He collapses to his knees and then falls to his back, crushing me between his bulk and the ground. I keep the cloth held over his face. His teeth are biting my palm through the material. Having rolled over to his front, he rears up to his feet. He staggers away with me clinging on to him. We are no longer hidden behind the van and are visible to any passing traffic. He topples forward and lands on his hands and knees. He proceeds to buck up and down, as if he were a bull at a rodeo and me the cowboy. A car is driving past. Two children and a woman are staring through its windows at us. The car speeds off.

Darko collapses onto his front and one arm flails out at his side. Finally, he is unconscious. After extracting the cloth from his purple-tinged face, I scramble to my feet and drag my forearm across my sweat-drenched forehead. He must be moved away from the road as more cars may come, including potentially the police car. I grip his thick ankles and drag him behind the van. I let go of his ankles, shove my forearms under his armpits, step up into the van and haul him through the open side door. He is incredibly heavy. I fall backwards to the floor. I clamber to my feet, jump out, snatch my gym bag from the front, climb in through the side door, and close it behind me.

I pull a length of rope from the gym bag, wrap it around his ankles and tie it tightly in a knot. Then I force an arm behind his back and rotate another piece of rope around his wrist. I am the process of securing the rope to his other wrist when he rolls onto his side, opens one bloodshot eye, and mutters, *'Jebi se. (Fuck you.)'*

He pulls his arm free, pushes me to the floor, sits up and pries at the knot around his ankles. I leap over him, grab a bottle of chloroform and a cloth from the gym bag, undo the bottle and empty some of the liquid on the cloth. The knot is partially undone and he is trying to free his foot. When I jump on him, he emits a loud, 'RAHH!'

The cloth is inserted over his mouth. He lets go of the rope and claws at the cloth. I push down with all my strength. His head slams on the floor. The cloth is left draped over his face. I pull the sofa on top of him, then refasten the knot around his ankles. He grips my ankle; I land on my posterior. His snarling face is edging towards me. I kick him. He yelps and releases his grip. I drag myself from the van, slide the side door shut and lock it.

I race around to the driver-side door, clamber in, stick the key in the ignition, start the engine, do a screeching hundred-and-eighty-degree turn, and drive off. He is bellowing and there are *crashing* noises. The police Volvo has been replaced by a police vehicle recovery lorry, which is in the process of hoisting the yellow car that was here earlier. I press the accelerator. Having turned onto the A335, I drive off in the direction of the airport. The entombed alleged war criminal is banging on the sides of the van. *BANG! BANG!*

'LET ME OUT!'

While steering one-handed, I telephone the contact number on my mobile phone. *Burrr, Burrr, Burrr … Come on. Burr—*

'Hello.'

'The police are still in the lay-by. I'm coming to you.'

'Impossible. No chance he agrees to come here to airport. We must wait for police to go or fi—'

'Listen! I have him locked up in my vehicle.' The banging intensifies. 'An airfield north end of the airport you said earlier. Are you still there?'

'Yes, airfield north part of airport. You will see a private jet parked. No other planes here.' *CRASH!* 'We have one of our people on the entrance gate. Tell him odmazda five. He will let you in.'

'On my way!'

CRASH! I hang up. *BANG!* He is either shoulder barging the sides of the van, or hurling objects against it. I need to get off the A335 quickly before drivers realise something is awry.

'STOP ...! STOP I SAID.' I press the accelerator. *'JEBI SE!'*

I am becoming rather familiar with this Serbian obscenity. On the right, there are several airfields. The last of them has a jet, possibly a Gulfstream, parked on its runway. I reach a roundabout. Having screeched around it, I accelerate towards the airfield. *CRASH!* To the left is a path with a sign that reads, 'No Unauthorised Traffic'. A spin of the steering wheel takes me onto the path. I bump to a halt in front of a fenced gate next to a portacabin. *BANG ...! BANG!*

'RAHH!'

The rental company will be unimpressed by the extensive damage his histrionics must be causing. A man in an orange jacket emerges from the portacabin. I unwind the window. *CRASH! CRASH!* My prisoner is ramming the sides of the van with such force that I am being shifted from side to side, and it feels as if the vehicle could topple over at any moment. The man is gawping at the rear of the van.

'Odmazda five.'

He scurries over to the fenced gate and opens it. I drive onto the runway and park beside the jet. Two burly men wearing sunglasses alight from the jet and trot down its steps.

'LET ME GO!' *BANG!* 'NOW!'

I climb out of the van and say, 'Good afternoon.'

One of the men points at the trembling van, and says, 'He in there?' I nod. The other man whips out what looks to be a cattle prod. 'Give me the key.'

I pass it to him. *BANG! BANG!* This rampage has indeed caused considerable denting. The man I gave the key to slips it into the side door's lock.

'LET ME GO, YOU POMPOUS FUCK!'

That is no way to address a superior. The man who inserted the key is holding three fingers aloft. He retracts them one by one. When the other man presses a switch on the prod, a blue current surges between its prongs. The door slides open and the man with the prod leaps inside.

'RAHH!' is followed in quick succession by a *crash*. On peering inside, I see my former employee convulsing on the floor with foam spewing from his lips. Handcuffs are fastened to Darko's wrists. The other man clambers in. He plants a knee on the captive, grabs his right hand, twists it, and inserts a blue-liquid-filled syringe into the underside of his forearm. Darko's body goes slack. A woman in a pleated skirt emerges with a stretcher. The unconscious war veteran is laid on the stretcher, fastened to it with straps, and carried off to the jet by the two men. The woman says, 'Come to the aircraft.'

I trot across the tarmac and up the steps to the jet. The interior is bedecked in beige leather upholstery. On the wall is a framed Croatian national football team shirt, covered in signatures. A white-haired man wearing spectacles is trotting towards me. He shakes my hand firmly, and says, 'Well done, you did a perfect job.'

'Yes, I did. In trying circumstances too.'

'You had a rough time, I see. You look about ready to die.'

'The Euros will recuperate me.'

'First, we must check him.'

The stretcher has been set down in the aisleway. The white-haired man is bent over it, examining the Serbian crest tattoo on the underside of my winning lottery ticket's left forearm. He prises Darko's mouth ajar and shines a torch into the cavity. The woman says, 'Can I get you a drink?'

'Yes, a glass of water please.'

This afternoon's rigours have left me feeling somewhat parched. I am reclining in a beige leather seat glugging water, when the white-haired man comes over to me with a briefcase. He places it on my lap. I open it. It is crammed with bundles of high denomination Euros.

'It is all there. If you want to check, please do.'

After counting the bundles, I extract a one hundred Euro banknote from the middle of a bundle, hold it up to the light, inspect the hologram, and feel the paper. This is bona fide. This procedure is repeated with half a dozen more banknotes. I say, 'A pleasure doing business with you.'

I close the briefcase. The white-haired man says, 'You have done an incredible job bringing him to us. With the police changing our plan last minute, it could have all gone wrong.'

'It certainly could have, but I came prepared.'

'So we see.' He points at the unconscious Darko lying on the stretcher on the floor. 'You have done a great thing. This man is very bad. He has a lot to answer for. Many of us suffered and continue to suffer because of the crimes he committed against us during the ...'

He is boring me. I say, 'That is our business concluded. Goodbye.'

I return to the van with the briefcase, which contains approximately two and a half decades worth of my Sunita-diminished salary. The rear resembles an upturned skip. A kitchen chair's seat has been separated from its legs, papers are strewn everywhere, and the walls, roof, and the inside of the sliding door are punctured with dents. Having turned the sofa the right way up, I stash the briefcase under one of its cushions, and then go through to the front. His purple anorak is still on the passenger seat. In a pocket, I find a wallet containing a twenty-pound note and a travel card, but no ID. On examining myself in the rear-view mirror, I see that my left eye is somewhat swollen. There is also a dull pain emanating from the front of my scalp, a result of him pulling my hair. I drive off.

While The Genocidal One has a surly manner and confrontational attitude, he possesses excellent taste in music and literature. It would have been infinitely preferable to exchange Sunita and/or Teleisha for the reward, though it is highly improbable that anyone would be willing to part with more than a handful of Euro coins for those two.

My intention was to return to London. However, the skirmish witnessed by the family at the lay-by, as well as potential prying motorists when I drove to the airfield, has changed the situation. This vehicle may have been reported to the police. If this is the case, it will inevitably be traced to Newton Van Hire, and ultimately to me. The van is registered in my name. Providing my driving licence and credit card details was a prerequisite for hiring it. As I may now require an alibi for being in this area, I decide to drive into the city of Southampton. En route, I check my mirrors frequently for police.

Having parked near the centre of Southampton, I change into the spare clothes that I brought along. On taking off my muddied chinos, I discover that one of my knees is grazed. Darko's anorak is dumped in a clothes recycle bank, his wallet in a bin. I come across a charity shop for the city's homeless. This would be an ideal place to dispose of some of the contents of the van. When I enter the premises, a middle-aged, councilesque woman wearing glasses and a floral-frock emerges from behind a desk.

'Can I help you?'

I explain that I am here to donate some furniture. She instructs a man to inspect it. Me and him go to the van, which is parked close by. He agrees to take the sofa and my kitchen chairs, other than the one that is severed in half. We carry them through to a storage area at the rear of the shop, then return to the van for the sofa. I have removed the briefcase from underneath the sofa's cushion and stashed it under some papers. Inside the shop, the woman thanks me for the furniture and offers me tea. I accept.

'How do you take it?'

'Milk and one sugar.'

On a desk there is a local newspaper, folded over at the sports section. I pick it up. The woman places a Styrofoam cup of tea in front of me, and says, 'Are you from around here?'

'No, I'm based in London.'

'Long way to come to deliver some chairs and a sofa.'

I have a sip of tea and peek at the newspaper. Southampton are playing Tottenham Hotspur at home tomorrow at twelve-thirty.

'I'm down here for the Southampton game tomorrow, amongst other things.'

'Oh, should be a good one. It's Spurs, isn't it?'

'Indeed, it is.'

'Big game, what with The Saints near the relegation zone. You're a Spurs fan then?'

'Yes, I am.'

She talks continuously. I hastily drink the tea and leave. After parking the van in a car park, I traipse around the Titanic Museum. I am in a Mexican restaurant drinking Corona beer when my mobile phone vibrates. I press the accept button.

'Forget me, bitch?'

'No. I do appreciate being add—'

'Where's the money at?'

136

'An instalment is on the way.'

'Nah, fuck that instalment shit. Pay up!'

'I will. But I am currently out of town.'

'Running from me?'

'No, certainly not. I will pay the money soon. Goodbye.'

Perhaps that ill-mannered reprobate takes Euros. I glug beer and ponder my situation. Driving from here to London with that briefcase of Euros would be folly, as there is a chance the police could stop me due to the earlier drama entailing The Genocidal One. They could conceivably search the vehicle and find the money. This potential problem could be avoided by making two trips.

In the van, I stuff the briefcase into my gym bag. I then venture into a McDonalds' toilet, where I put on a wind proofer and a red Reebok baseball cap which I brought with me on the trip. I walk to the train station and buy a ticket from the machine with cash. On the London Waterloo-bound train, I stay hidden for the duration of the journey behind a newspaper. At Waterloo, I catch the bus to Newton Central and then travel on foot to Newton Old Cemetery. I switch on my Nokia's flashlight and weave amongst the graves to the far end of the cemetery, where there is a tomb I am familiar with, which has a hole at one end. The gym bag is crammed into the hole and lowered into the tomb.

I take the bus to Waterloo and the train to Southampton. Having jettisoned the baseball cap and wind proofer, I go to a bar. There I make the acquaintance of two female students from the university. We drink Tequila shots until the early hours, and then head to their residence where I spend the night. The following day, I go to the football stadium and purchase a ticket for the game off a lout in a Burberry jacket. After the game I drive to London in the rental van. The papers and publications I brought along to dupe Darko are dumped at a recycling plant on the way.

TWELVE

THAT EVENING – Ristorante Toscana – A waitress comes over and says, '*Signore e signora*, are you ready to order drinks?'

I say, '*Due bicchieri di chianti e una bottiglia di acqua minerale.*'

'You speak Italian,' says Rakesha. 'That's so romantic.'

'Romance is my middle name.'

Following a giggle, Rakesha unravels her napkin and places it on her lap. My mobile phone vibrates. I slip it out of my trouser pocket and inspect the screen underneath the table.

....

Today 19:23

Hiya, Hope you're enjoying your weekend. Can't wait to see you. Not long to go! Thank you so much for everything you've done for me. I appreciate it SO much! ☺

Eva xxxx

....

I return the device to my pocket. Rakesha says, 'The music is lovely. Guess it must be Italian.'

'This is *Tosca*.'

'*Tosca?*'

'*Tosca* is an opera written by the Tuscany-born composer and avid wildfowler, Giacomo Puccini.'

'Wildfowler?'

'Someone who hunts wild birds.'

'That's so cruel.'

Rakesha impales a white *cannelloni* bean on her fork. I take a sip from my glass of Chianti. She looks at me with her large hazel eyes and twirls a length of brown curly hair in her fingertip. Rakesha proceeds to stroke my leg under the table with a stockinged foot. I have a bite of *prosciutto*; she has a nibble of *bruschetta*.

This afternoon I went for a jog. I was cantering along a street not far from my abode, when I came across the soon-to-be deceased dealer and his posse on the other side of the street. With the fading light and my tracksuit hood pulled up, pursuing them was simple. The posse's destination was the Hope Court address. While they were inside the flat, I did some circuits of the grassed area outside the building. Ten minutes had elapsed when they exited the address, with the exception of my target.

'What happened to your eye?'

'One of my employees struck me with a rake.'

'Oh my God, that must have hurt. It was an accident, right?'

'Yes. But if he does it again, I will fire him.'

Rakesha giggles, which causes her to splutter on her Chianti. Once I have my kit assembled, it will be simple enough to pole up at the address when I know he is alone. I will tell him that I have come to pay off the debt. If he enquires as to how I knew he would be here, I will tell him Eva told me where he lived.

The main courses arrive. Mine is *pappardelle al cinghiale*.

The pasta is *al dente,* the meat is cooked to perfection. Rakesha dips her fork into her risotto and raises it to her mouth.

'Yummy. How's yours?'

'Mine is good.'

'Love pappardelle pasta. What meat is in it?'

'Cinghiale.' She raises her eyebrows. 'Wild boar.'

'Oh, nice.'

It is doubtful that The Genocidal One is dining on *pappardelle al cinghiale* tonight.

'Ha.'

'Something funny?'

'No.'

Having dabbed her lips with her napkin, she says, 'It's about time I told you a little bit about me. My dad's from Antigua and my mum's from Leeds. She moved back there when they split up. Dad went back to the island.' I paw the monocle in my trouser pocket. 'Seven years ago it was. Time flies.' She has a sip of Chianti. 'So, familywise in London these days, it's just my daughter Shaneeka and my sister who lives close by. Which is a godsend ...' She puts a forkful of risotto into her mouth, swallows, fixes her hazel eyes on my face, and continues talking. 'As for my future plans, professional wise I want to stay at the council and progress there. And as for homelife, I would like to have another child. A brother or sister for my daughter.' To my left, I can see a trolley containing desserts. There is a tiramisu, a *panna cotta,* profiteroles, and a *torta di mandorle.* Italian almond cake. 'So yeah, if I was to get into a relationship again that is what I would be looking for.'

I nod. Rakesha evidently likes the sound of her own voice. If I had invited Kei along, the evening would have been more entertaining. However, Rakesha is seemingly too self-obsessed to accommodate her. Whatever activities she has planned for post-dinner must be concluded by ten-thirty, as there is a programme on about the Napoleonic Wars which I am loath to miss.

*

15:32 – The next day – I am on my way to pay a further instalment to Eva's irascible dealer. It should stop him chasing me for a while. The next time we meet will be when I pole up at his flat when he is there alone. I did not text him on this occasion, as it is for the best that traceable communication with him is kept to a minimum, considering what is poised to occur. Pegasus is on top of the skateboard ramp, surrounded by the posse. His accomplice is there, three other young men, the two girls I have seen with him previously, and the mastiff. Even from this distance Pegasus appears weedy. Overpowering him will be mere child's play compared to grappling with that veteran of the Yugoslav Wars. One of the girl's points at me, and calls out, 'It's the fit man, looks like James Bond.'

Having exclaimed, 'Shut the fuck up, ho!' Pegasus leaps off the skateboard ramp and struts over to me. 'What's up, bitch?'

'Good afternoon to you too.'

I fix my gaze on the stumpy dreadlock entwined with yellow, green and red cotton at the front of his head. It is destined for my fly-fishing tin.

'What you looking at? Where's the dough?'

I extract my wallet and remove the two-hundred-and-fifty-pounds that I got from the cashpoint on the way here.

'Here it is.'

'Nah, all of it!'

'This is what I have today. The remainder will be paid in due course.'

'You deaf?' He snatches the money off me. 'Said all of it. Ain't a mortgage. Done with this shit. Pay up!'

'I will next time.'

Pegasus grins, revealing a mouth crammed with glittering, gold capped teeth. He claps and shouts, 'Gather round!'

The posse charge over, the accomplice leading the way. He

141

is wearing a T-shirt with the image of a handgun emblazoned across the front. It is time to leave.

'Our business is concluded for today. Goodbye.'

When I swivel around, he says, 'Not going nowhere, bitch. Pay up!'

Pegasus pushes me meagrely. The posse surrounds me. The mastiff growls; one of the girl's giggles. With my palms held out in front of me, I say, 'We have been through this. I will pay the debt imminently. Imminently means soon.'

'Fuck dat! Pay nah!'

'No.'

'Take him down!'

Two of the young men grip me by the arms and the accomplice punches me in the stomach. I drop to my knees. Someone barges me from behind. I fall forward to the ground. The snarling mastiff plants a paw on my shoulder. Drool spills from its jaws onto my jacket. Pegasus kicks me in the ribs.

'Pay up by end of play next week.' He sticks two fingers into the side of my head. 'Or *bang bang*, you and your bitch.'

The posse erupts in laughter. I rise to my knees. A foot in my back pushes me over again. The laughter intensifies. One of the girls has an extremely loud, high-pitched shrieking laugh that dominates the others. I hold my hands to my ears and close my eyes. Cousin and nemesis Beatrice appears before me. Its pigtails are dangling menacingly from the sides of its head and it is laughing raucously. To the accompaniment of Beatrice's high-pitched, shrieking laughter, I am hoisted up by the bevy of school children and carried off to the toilets. When I open my eyes, the posse have disappeared.

*

Twenty hours later – 'You've got your actual expenses and your budget here,' says the head of finance, who is leaning his skinny

142

frame over my shoulder as he inspects the Sage financial report on my computer screen. 'And you have your actual YTD, the budget YTD, and the variance. Let me check the figures.' He clicks my mouse on a variance field. 'Perfect. A Sage expert is what you are.' He taps me on the shoulder. 'Impressive stuff.'

I know. He walks off. Teleisha is staring at me. When I make eye contact with it, it looks away. In the not-too-distant future, I will be quitting the council. However, not quite yet. The authorities could potentially learn of Darko's disappearance. And if they learn who he is, they might suspect I was involved in his abduction, if that is they are made aware that I was meeting with him last Friday. Rakesha is beside my desk. She bends over and whispers in my ear, 'Friday night was amazing. You're so hot.'

Having winked at me, she totters off. Meagre Martin scurries over and deposits some items of post and December's issue of *Morgue Monthly* in my in tray. I pluck it from the in tray and rip off its transparent plastic, protective cover. A packet is being opened. When I look up, I see a fistful of Monster Munches being shoved into the cavernous crevice that serves as Teleisha's mouth.

'Eating is prohibited in Burials and Cemeteries, as you well know.'

Two slits submerged in a fat face glare at me. It lurches out of its chair and waddles off in the direction of the kitchen. As is to be expected from a publication with a readership consisting of death business personnel, *Morgue Monthly* is industry specific and technical. Topics include insurance provision, health and safety regulations, and product reviews. There are a multitude of advertisements for everything from cremators and hearses, to morgue fridges and harnesses for lifting the deceased.

As Darren strolls past my desk, he points at my left eye, and blurts, 'Shiner!'

There is an email from Rebecca, informing me how *pleasant*

it was to walk into Boden this morning and find no Kiro there. She has attached a photograph of herself, Cheikh and Angus, taken by the Crimean War memorial obelisk. They are sporting wide grins and have their thumbs raised. It is remarkable that the trio are in such celebratory mood, considering they did not receive a single Euro for his departure.

'Dyson, what's so funny?'

Frank is by my desk. I say, 'A work-related matter. It would take a while to explain.' When I twist towards him, a jolt of pain emanates from my left ribs. 'Ah!'

'Everything alright?'

'I'm fine.'

'You sure? You went *ah* and you grimaced.'

'Just a tight muscle is all.'

'You've got a bit of a black eye there. Been in the wars, you have.' He glances at his wrist. 'Running late, got to shoot. We should play another round of golf sometime if you're up for it?'

'Count me in.'

'Will get back to you on that. Catch you in a bit.'

Pegasus will pay dearly for bruising my ribs and attempting to humiliate me. The mode of execution will be personal. It is time to assemble my kill kit. Another trip to Raven & Co. Funeral Directors is in order. There is no time like the present.

*

When Fraser opens the door, I say, 'Good afternoon.'

'Dyson, what a surprise! Actually, it's not that much of a surprise. You are prone to poling up here unannounced.' He steps to the side. 'Come on in.' I enter the premises. 'Golf trip to Argyll was quite something. I say golf. We ended up doing more drinking than golf.' We go through to the mortuary. 'Sally's off today and it's chaos here. Admin and me just don't go together. I wouldn't survive long without her.'

Good. If his secretary is not in today, it will make it easier to plunder the mortuary shelves. Fraser passes me a résumé with a passport-sized photograph clipped to it, of a blond man with chiselled features.

'He looks like that eighties film star from the He-Man film.'

'Dolph Lungren. The movie is called *Masters of the Universe*.' Fraser grabs a makeup brush from a mortuary shelf and brandishes it two-handed above his head. 'I have the power!'

'Yes, I remember the film from my youth. It is particularly poor.'

'I must break you,' he says in a Russian accent. 'That's from *Rocky IV*. Guess which Lundgren movie this one's from? Say good night, asshole.' I shrug my shoulders. '*Universal Soldier*.' He prods at the résumé I am holding. 'Dolph Lungren lookalike Attila Kiprich studied chemistry at Budapest University then did an MSc in embalming. He professes to be something of a waterless embalming expert. You wouldn't find anyone his age so well qualified in the UK these days.'

'Attila sounds promising then.'

'Fluent in five languages.' He prods at the résumé. 'Check out his interests at the bottom of the page. Bench-pressing. He told me he benched five-hundred-and-fifty pounds raw at the Hungarian Nationals. No idea what raw means, but that's a hell of a weight. In kilos, it's about, um, two hundred and something.'

'Two hundred and fifty approximately.'

'Atilla is just like Dolph, and not just in appearance. He's strong, smart, and no doubt can't act for shit.' There is a ringing noise. Fraser removes a telephone from the breast pocket of his white mortuary apron. 'Good afternoon, Raven & Co. Funeral Directors ... I will check our diary. Please hold for a moment while I go through to the office.'

Having pressed a button on the device, he says, 'When I've dealt with this client, I'll show you the new arrival.' He gestures with a tilt of his head at the mortuary fridge. 'Victim of a bus

145

and moped collision. There's no prize for guessing which she was driving. Bit of a black eye there. One of your women finally had enough of your shtick?'

'No, it was a result of a minor collision.'

'Not a bus and a moped then.'

The moment he leaves the mortuary, I slip the gym bag off my shoulder and peruse the supplies. Dyes, humectants make-up, Restoria, shampoos, boxes of tissues, plastic eye caps. None of these will be of any use. Bolt gun, water correctors and arterial conditioners. No, no, and no.

These bottles all contain cavity chemicals. Pouring them into that ex-child soldier's orifices could be highly entertaining. However, it might not be effective. Mortuary gloves. Yes, two pairs of those. These white, disposable all-in-one body suits could come in useful. Masks; yes. Formaldehyde, where are you …? There you are. A bottle will suffice. And a syringe to administer it. I rub my palms together. Up close and personal; this is going to be fun. Scalpels are not necessary. Well, they could come in useful for severing off my memento. But a knife will suffice. I am zipping up the gym bag when Fraser's head emerges through the mortuary door.

'I fight to win, for me! FOR ME!'

*

Business jargon is a clear and present danger to the English language. Take the citizen empowerment meeting that I am presently leaving. Linguistic faecal matter such as re-baselining, mainstreaming, beacon, synergies, best practice, thinking outside of the box, upstream, and actioned have no place in the English language, or any language for that matter.

On the way to the lifts, a female finance department employee, says, 'Hey Dyson, feeling synergised?'

'Certainly not.'

146

'*He*, that makes two of us.'

Outside the lifts, a man, possibly education, says, 'Dyson, you about to baseline the mainstream to Burials and Cemeteries?'

'No, I am taking the lift there.'

'Haha, good answer. Like that.'

Having deposited myself on the revolving office chair, I stifle a yawn with the back of my hand. Last night, I did not get a great deal of sleep. Considerable time was spent watching the Hope Court address from the grassed area in front of it. Several minutes before midnight, Pegasus emerged from his flat. I watched him strut along the illuminated landing, jog down the external stairs, and disappear into the darkness. Some youths were loitering in the grassed area, and as I did not wish to draw attention to myself, I departed.

When I returned twenty minutes later, the youths were gone. Shortly thereafter, Pegasus materialised with a girl from his posse. They went into the flat. Ten minutes had elapsed when the girl reappeared alone. I was poised to go to my abode to collect my kill kit when the youths came back. They proceeded to drink, smoke and chatter. One of their number asked me what I was doing. I returned to my flat and promptly went to sleep, only to be awakened by the recurring nightmare featuring nemesis Beatrice.

I recline in the revolving office chair and paw the earring in my left trouser pocket. At the same time, I drum the fingers of my right hand on the chair's arm. As I do so, I picture my Euro-filled future. When I close my eyes, I see myself sitting on the terrace of a restaurant overlooking the sea. On the table in front of me is a book, a glass of white wine, and a platter of seafood containing lobster, prawns, red snapper, and an assortment of other grilled fish.

'Did you watch *X Factor* last night?'

I grit my teeth. That was HR's Emma speaking to Teleisha.

'Yeah, crazy it was. Still can't believe she was voted out.'

'That makes two of us. Was sure she'd win the whole thing.'

'Me too. Think half the country was …'

The mere mention of that ghastly programme in my department should result in disciplinary measures. I get up and have a stroll around the office. Council workers are huddled chattering around a photocopier. If I were to pole up here in ten, twenty, or even thirty years' time, it would be the same scene. The printer would have changed. It will be more streamlined, have a wider array of features, will print in more vivid colours, and at a quicker speed. But the council workers will still be dressed in dreary garb, clasping mugs of tea, and discussing their abject affairs and other mundane matters.

I have taken the afternoon off. As my resignation from the council is imminent, I might as well use up some of my remaining annual leave. I left the office at the stroke of midday and went to the centre of town, where I changed some Euros at a Bureau de Change, that I retrieved from the tomb last night. For lunch, I dined on *moules mariniéres* in Covent Garden. After lunch, I perused the shelves of the Borders bookshop on Tottenham Court Road. Two purchases were made – *La Planète des Singes*. *Planet of the Apes* in English. And *Le Pont de la Rivière Kwai*, or *Bridge over the River Kwai*. Both titles were penned by Pierre Boulle.

Currently, I am in my flat having a siesta on the sofa in the living room. I sit up and commence reading *La Planète des Singes*. The story is about three human explorers who travel to a planet where the roles have been reversed. Great apes are the dominant species and humans exist as primitive non-civilised creatures. They are probably no different to many of the council workers who plague my office. I rest the book on my lap and give some thought as to what will transpire tonight.

It is ill-advisable to be lingering outside in possession of my kill kit, and I do not want to have to return to my flat for it, in the off chance that in the intervening period, Pegasus either leaves the premises, or receives visitors, as was the case last night. Due to this consideration, I have just borrowed a car from an elderly neighbour of Eva's, who I am acquainted with. I told him that I needed it to move *some things* from Eva and my respective flats. The car is an old, rusting Mini Metro on its last legs. However, it fits my requirements. It will be parked in an unlighted area close to Hope Court. The kill kit can be easily retrieved from it when I am ready to execute.

It is 23:47, and I am going through the supplies for later, which are laid out on the floor. Disposable all-in-one mortuary suit, two pairs of mortuary gloves, mask, swimming goggles, three bottles of bleach, bottle of formaldehyde, syringe, plastic sheeting, plastic bags, saw, three knives, bin liners, Blu Tack, pliers ... Having changed into the all-in-one mortuary body suit, I put on a tracksuit over it. There is a documentary on television about the Spanish Civil War. I watch it.

At 00:13 I exit my building and head off into the darkness with the hood of my tracksuit pulled up. The Mini Metro is parked close by. I stash the spacious, wheeled expandable zip-up bag containing my supplies on the back seats, and then clamber into the front. After parking the Mini Metro in the pre-arranged spot, I make my way to the grassed area with the uninterrupted view of Hope Court. The youths from last night are not here. The wind is rustling in the trees behind me. It starts raining. Time passes.

A motorbike is being revved in the parking area outside Hope Court. I can see the outline of someone stumbling across the grass. I crouch down. They stumble over to Hope Court, ascend the external stairs, stumble along the first-floor landing and disappear into a flat. Number seventeen's lights are off. Pegasus could be inside. However, I suspect he isn't, or a light would probably be on. His line of work does not lend itself to early nights. It is now 00:29. I could collect my kit and knock on his door. If he is in, and alone, I would proceed with the plan. If someone else is there, I could give him some of the money and leave. But the most likely scenario is that he is not in. As I ponder the situation, I nibble on my left little finger's fingernail. If he is not in, it would then be a matter of coming again tomorrow. Thirteen minutes have passed when I hear voices in the darkness behind me. I crouch.

'Wah gwan?'

'Watch him! He's vexed, innit?'

That was Pegasus. Colloquial nonsense, as to be expected. On the grass I can see the outlines of three people and a large dog. The quartet stroll through the darkness towards Hope Court. Moments later they appear at the bottom of the external stairs. Three disperse, the other hurtles up the stairs. I watch Pegasus disembark on the second floor, strut along the landing, and enter his flat. It's on. I dash to the Mini Metro, clamber in and unzip the expandable zip-up bag. I put a mask, swimming goggles and a cloth in the left pocket of my tracksuit top, along with a wad of cash. The pre-prepared syringe filled with formaldehyde is packed in a plastic case. Cotton wool has been placed over the needle to prevent spillage. I tuck the case in the right pocket of my tracksuit top. I put on the gloves, grab the bag containing my supplies, then check the mirrors for approaching pedestrians and vehicles.

After edging around the side of the building, I stop at the bottom of the external stairs. There is no noise coming from above. I ascend to floor two. The lights in the nearest flat to the stairs are on and there is the sound of a television coming from inside. I duck below the window, creep past the property, stand up and continue along the landing to number seventeen. I display the banknotes in my gloved left hand in a fan shape. Following a deep inhalation of air through my nose, I position myself in front of the doorway and press the buzzer. Footsteps are audible. They stop. I smile and hold up the money. The door flies open.

'What you doing at my manor?'

'I have come to clear the outstanding debt.'

He snatches the money from me.

'Ain't all of it. Where's the rest at, fool?'

'I have it with me. Perhaps we should do this inside.'

He prods me in the chest and spits, 'How you know I was here?'

'I didn't. Eva told me where you lived. I came on the off chance you were here.'

'Phone first! Basic manners, innit? Don't be poling up unannounced. Get people shook with dat shit.'

'Shook?'

'Nervous, on edge. Don't you speak English?'

'I speak English. This was a surprise visit.'

'Fuck surprises!' He cranes his neck forward and looks left and right. 'Step inside.' I pick up the bag and step into the property. 'Stop!' Having set the bag down on the linoleum floor, I peer into the gloomy interior of a living room. The only illumination is being discharged from a lava lamp. There is the acrid odour of cannabis smoke. Pegasus closes the door. 'Show me the dough!'

'Do you take Euros?'

'Fuck I do.'

'Didn't think so.'

'Why you asking then? Street today you! Where's your dapper shit? Suit 'n all.'

'I didn't want my suit to get stained?'

'Stained. What you talking about, chief? 'N you've got gloves on. Kitchen gloves or some shit.' He shoves the bag beside me with his foot. ''N you brought a suitcase. Ain't a hotel, you get me? Show it! What you waiting for?'

When I remove the wad of banknotes, Pegasus grins, revealing gold-capped teeth. If I was not set on that dreadlock, a tooth would be a suitable memento. He grabs the money off me, bows his head and proceeds to count it at a rapid pace. For several seconds, I stand watching my dangling memento. He is halfway through counting the wad when I punch him on the side of his head.

'AHH!' It falls to the floor, reaches to the back of its trousers, and pulls out the handgun with the engraved stock. I drop my knee on its chest and twist its wrist. The handgun falls from its grip. 'You're dead, fool!' I grasp a handful of dreadlocks and smash its head on the floor. '*Basta-dog!*' It gropes at my face. I push its forearms to the side and headbutt its chin. I then knock its head on the floor several times. It makes a 'Mmm' noise and goes limp.

While kneeling astride of it, I haul the cloth from my pocket and stuff it in its mouth. Bulging eyes stare up at me. It writhes about, pushes my stomach meagrely with one hand, and reaches with the other for the handgun which is lying on the floor beside it. While continuing to straddle it, I watch its futile efforts to escape. Its fingertips clasp the handgun's stock. I clench onto its wrist and bang its knuckles on the linoleum floor. It makes a 'Mahh' noise and releases its grip on the stock. Again, it reaches for the handgun, and again I allow it to touch the stock before hitting its wrist on the floor. The routine is repeated three further times. This cat-and-mouse-style game is fun. It makes another grab for the handgun; I reach out and push it away. It tries to spit the cloth from its mouth. 'P-p-p.' The heels of its trainer-clad feet tap the linoleum floor repeatedly. *Tap, tap, tap …*

When it tries to buck me off, I place my palms on the floor to maintain my balance. I slam its head on the floor. It goes limp. Formaldehyde is extremely toxic, so I take the swimming goggles and mask from my bag and put them on. It regains consciousness. When it resumes struggling, I kneel on it. A right hook to the face and it goes limp. Blood is trickling from one of its nostrils. After pinning its left arm under my knee, I remove the plastic case from the pocket of my tracksuit top. The syringe is extracted, and the cotton wool pried from the tip of the needle. It is bucking once more, clawing at my chest and trying to spit the cloth from its mouth.

'P-p-p.'

As the needle descends, it stares up at me wide-eyed and squirms frantically. The needle pierces its left eye. It grips my wrist with both its hands and pushes up. I punch the tip of its nose. It releases its grasp. The point of the needle is angled upwards towards its brain. There is a *squelch* as the needle passes through the pupil. I push down on the plunger, releasing the noxious, highly toxic contents. Its body convulses violently for several seconds. The spasms become feebler; the body goes slack. The syringe is protruding from its left eye. I yank the cloth from its mouth and then wrest the membrane-smeared syringe free.

The corpse is dragged by its ankles through to the bathroom, where it is deposited headfirst over the side of the bath. I collect my bag from the living room. The plastic sheeting that I brought with me is draped over the bathroom's floor and walls. Its clothes have been taken off, apart from its Calvin Klein briefs. I was loath to remove them. Everything has been stashed in plastic bags and dumped in the living room. I have taken off the tracksuit and am wearing the disposable all-in-one mortuary suit with its hood pulled up, along with the mask and gloves. Plastic bags are tied over my feet. Having sawed off my memento with a serrated kitchen knife, I hold it up to the light and examine the stumpy dreadlock, entwined with yellow, green and red cotton.

I slit the throat from ear to ear. A gurgling precedes a gush of dark red blood spurting into the bathtub and splattering its sides. The gush diminishes to a trickle. While I wait for it to drain, I watch television in the living room. There is a programme on about a recent Cretan archaeological dig, in which a substantial amount of pottery was discovered, including several ornate jugs. When I return to the bathroom, the trickle has reduced to a steady drip.

I position its neck over the side of the bath, push down on the head and saw near the top of the spine at the cervical curvature. *SsSsSsSsSs* ... Tiny shards of bone cascade into the bathtub. The head is connected to the body by only a thin length of spine. Its head is rotated clockwise. The bone *cracks* and *snaps*. I hold the head aloft and inspect it in the mirror above the sink. This would make an excellent Halloween party prop. Sunita would no doubt disapprove. The right eye is half open, the left tumescent and discoloured. Its tongue is lolling from the corner of its mouth. The length of spine is jutting out from the bottom of its neck. I place the head in the basin, with the splintered spine shaft inserted in the plughole, so that it can view its body being dismembered.

After slicing through the flesh at the top of the leg to the bone, I press my weight on the leg and start sawing. *SsSsSs* ... The leg snaps off and falls on the plastic sheeting-covered floor. Next up is the other leg. This saw, with its bendy blade, is wholly inadequate. *SsSsSs* ... Time for the arms. I cut through the skin and tendons. This arm contains remarkably little blood, a result of it having been removed from the body and no longer being supplied by the heart. These are very puny arms. All sinew and devoid of even a semblance of muscle. While using the saw, I address the head in the basin.

'You really should work out.' *SsSsSs* ... 'There is an effective workout routine I do and would highly recommend.' *SsSsSs* 'It is ideal for functional muscle development. Five or six body-weight exercises are performed one after the other without rest. Press ups ...'

The clean-up operation takes over an hour. There are body parts to wrap, tools to clean, and plastic sheeting to be folded up. The bath and the basin are scrubbed with bleach, and the floor in the living room wiped. After dragging everything through to the living room, I return to the bathroom and carefully check it. Forgetting anything on occasions such as this is ill-advised. It is imperative to get it right the first time. I crawl around the room, checking for bone splinters and droplets of blood. I find none. The bathroom is far too pristine compared to the rest of the property, which is relatively dirty. This could potentially arouse suspicion. I put on a clean pair of mortuary gloves. A dustpan and brush are used to collect dust from shelves and the tops of cupboards. The dust is sprinkled around the bathroom.

A thorough inspection of the property would reveal blood in the bath and basin's pipework. However, there is nothing to suggest to the police that the former child soldier is dead. And even if they eventually suspect that it is dead, they will not assume that it was executed, decapitated and dismembered in its own residence. A search of the property unearths two thousand pounds in cash, five small bags of cocaine, several ounces of weed, some grams of heroin, half a dozen rocks of crack, and an assortment of multi-coloured pills. One thousand pounds is acquisitioned. The remainder of the money and the drugs will be left here. If the posse gain entry to the flat, there is nothing to suggest that their irksome leader was the victim of a robbery. It will be as if it disappeared into thin air.

This assignment has been executed with aplomb. Having taken a moment to congratulate myself, I stuff everything into the expandable zip-up bag. The last item to pack is the head. There is not enough space for it in the bag. I rearrange the contents, to no avail. The head is stashed in a wardrobe in the bedroom. I will return for it. The handgun is tucked in the waistband of my tracksuit bottoms. Its mobile phone is in the kitchen. There are three missed calls. I switch off the device, pocket it along with its house key, open the front door and peek out. I would prefer not to be seen dragging this suspicious looking bag. There is no one on the landing, so I make a dash for it, dragging the heavy, wheeled expandable bag behind me.

After loading the bag into the Mini Metro, I go to collect the head. Three youths have emerged on the landing. They are chatting and smoking. For ten minutes, I wait on the grassed area in front of Hope Court for them to depart. However, they do not. Four figures convene close to where I am. They are evidently inebriated and in no hurry to leave. It is too risky waiting any longer. I will return for the head tomorrow.

THIRTEEN

O8:22 – THE NEXT MORNING – Bellucci's Café – Newton High Street – I say, 'No, not a sesame roll. I want a crusty roll, as I have already informed you.'

'No have.'

I peer into the basket containing rolls behind the counter. There are four varieties, but no crusty rolls.

'You have always had crusty rolls when I have come here previously.' The man looks at me and blinks. 'You can't tell me you've sold out already. This place only opened at eight.'

'I check back.'

'You do that.'

Moments later he returns, shrugs, and says, 'We not have.'

'In that case I will have a wholemeal roll ... Not that roll, it's white. I said wholemeal. Yes, that's the one. And an apple juice.'

Coffee can wait. I will be getting my usual takeaway from Starbucks post breakfast. I stifle a yawn with my sleeve. It was a long night. Ideally, I would have a few more hours sleep before going into work. However, I am a consummate professional and a poor night's sleep will not prevent me from fulfilling my duties. The body is still in the Mini Metro. Once I have the head, I will dispose of it.

*

08:57 – Having switched on my office computer, I take a sip from my caffè latte extra hot with soya milk. Frank is hurrying along the passageway. He stops adjacent to my desk and tightens his maroon tie.

'Morning, Dyson.'

'Good morning.'

'How's things?'

'I'm doing well.'

'Good stuff. Have a full-on day today. Got to fly, have a meeting starting at nine. We'll get a date in the diary for the golf. See you later.'

He hurries off. I read Teleisha's subpar responses to emails from my department's inbox. HR's Emma is chatting near the printer. She is far too close to my department for my liking. Moments later, she trespasses into Burials and Cemeteries. An electrified, razor wire perimeter fence is the solution.

'Hi Dyson.'

'Good morning.'

'You have to see this!' She presses a mobile phone at me. 'Isn't it just the cutest thing ever?' There is a photograph on the screen of a small boy, hanging from a climbing frame. 'My five-year-old. He looks just like a little monkey, doesn't he?'

He does. It's the face. She retracts the device and moves away. My impending, council worker-free existence is going to be immensely satisfactory. I continue reading the subpar email responses. A tremoring floor precedes the arrival of Teleisha. It collapses onto its chair and emits a lengthy sigh. I wait a minute for its computer to load then say, 'Open the email you sent at 10:32 yesterday to the community group, Friends of Boden Cemetery.'

'Got it up. What of it?'

'Firstly, organisation has an S in it, not a Z. This isn't America.'

Replicating that nation's obesity fad is one thing, but I will not tolerate the defilement of my once proud nation's language.

'And?'

'A more emphatic closing statement was needed. Yours was ambiguous.' I point at it. 'A challenge for you. Over the course of this morning, you will come up with some alternative closing statements. You can run them past me after lunch.'

'That it?'

'Yes, that will be all.'

Following a grunt, it heaves itself from its chair and waddles off. It's kitchen bound. I feel the stumpy dreadlock in the left-side pocket of my suit jacket. Having pulled it up to the mouth of the pocket, I examine the elaborate braid, entwined with yellow, green and red cotton. Harvesting it was a tiring and time-consuming business, but an immensely satisfactory one. Through the corner of my eye, I see Rakesha tottering over. I release my grip on my new memento. What an overpowering aroma. She must have doused herself from top to toe in perfume. Rakesha crouches next to my chair.

'Hey.'

'Good morning.'

She whispers in my ear, 'Let's have lunch soon. Somewhere Darren won't find us.'

'Yes, let's.'

After caressing my shoulder, she leaves Burials and Cemeteries. The lunch will be the opportune moment to tell her that I am only prepared to keep seeing her on a casual basis. Rakesha might become angry and create a scene, but it is preferable that she does so in a restaurant and not in the office. I resume fiddling with my memento. Meagre Martin is pushing a trolley along the passageway. It has a Harley-Davidson logo sticker plastered to it. I can hear him talking to a council worker about his visit to an American-style pit stop café last night. I pluck the memento from my pocket and rotate it in my fingertips. The telephone on my desk is ringing. I place the dreadlock in my pocket and answer it.

'Good morning, Burials and Cemeteries.'

'Dyson, Sunita here. Come up to my office, now!'

Contemptuous creature that Sunita. Fortunately, it will soon be reduced to a bitter memory. I ascend the stairs to floor eight. Through the glass wall of its office, three people are visible. It and two men. The men are wearing white shirts and dark waistcoats. As I draw closer, I see that they are holding flat hats with bibs. These are not council workers, they are police. What do they want from me? Is this a cemetery-related matter? Vandalism perhaps, drug use, or prostitution. Or is their presence here to do with Darko. It surely can't be Pegasus related. They will not be aware anything untoward has happened to that irksome dealer. As I approach the office, I murmur, *Cemetery related, cemetery related. Be cemetery related.* I knock on the glass door, open it, and say, 'Good morning.'

The policemen twist their heads and look at me. Sunita's eyes are bulging in the manner of a deep-sea fish, which has been dragged up too quickly from the depths. It says, 'They're here to see you.'

I tilt my palms upwards, smile, and say, 'How can I be of assistance?'

The policeman on the right says, 'We are here about one of your staff.' *Damn!* 'Kiro Burgan.'

The two policemen are watching me intently. I smile faintly, maintain eye contact with them, and say, 'What about him?'

'He has gone missing.'

'How unfortunate,' is coordinated with a horizontal sweep of my hand with the palm facing down. 'Kiro is no longer employed in my department. He was only a temporary employee. Might I suggest that you contact the employment agency he was hired from. They may be able to assist.' I extend my arm towards Sunita, who is glaring at me with its bulging fish eyes from behind its desk. 'If my colleague has not already provided you with the agency in question's details, I would be happy to do so.'

The policeman on the left says, 'That won't be necessary. We have some questions for you. We would like you to come with us to the station, voluntarily of course, to answer these questions.'

'Certainly. I am keen to help.'

As I exit the office, Sunita spits, 'You've got some explaining to do!'

It is high time that red *bindi* dot tremors and the back of its head explodes. Rakesha and two other council workers are in the foyer. As I stride past them, she stares at me with her mouth agape. On the way to the police station, I comment on the weather. Someone must have reported him missing. The police presumably know something about his last known movements, or I wouldn't be here. In situations such as this, it is best to tell the truth, and only lie when it is strictly necessary. Muffled talking is audible on one of the policemen's radios. I paw the memento in my suit jacket pocket. In the police station's entrance, there is a Nescafé vending machine.

'I bet the coffee from your machine is better than the coffee dispensed by the machine at the council.' The policemen glance at each other. They say nothing. 'I will grab a cappuccino.'

This is vastly superior to the swill masquerading as cappuccino, the machine on floor eight stocks. One of the policemen accompanies me along a corridor to a brightly lit interview room. A suited woman is sitting behind a desk. She is in her mid-thirties and has brown hair drawn tightly in a bun. She says, 'Thank you for coming, Mr Devereux.'

'Glad to be of assistance.'

'I'm Inspector Pascal. Please take a seat.' I sit down on a chair on the other side of the desk to her and the policeman who came in with me. Pascal's beady eyes fix on me. 'We have some questions regarding Mr Burgan. He has been reported missing.'

161

'So I gathered.'

'Before we begin, a few formalities. Do you have any known physical or mental issues?'

'No.'

'Have you consumed alcohol or drugs in the last twenty-four hours?'

'No.'

'Do you require help with reading or writing, or have any learning difficulties?'

'Certainly not.'

After explaining that the interview will be recorded, she states the date and time, and then presses a button on a recording device.

'You do not have to say anything, but it may harm your defence if you do not mention when questioned something which you later rely on in court. Anything you do say may be given in evidence. You are not under arrest, and you are free to leave at any point. Is that understood?'

'Yes.'

'In what capacity do you know Kiro Burgan?'

'Work. He was employed as a cemeteries and parks maintenance person. I am Head of Burials and Cemeteries.'

'When did you last see Mr Burgan?'

They must know something about his movements, or I wouldn't be here. I go with, 'Last Friday at approximately three o'clock.'

'Where were you?'

'On the edge of Southampton.'

She rests her elbows on the desk and presses the fingertips of both hands together.

'What were you doing there?'

'I was driving to Southampton.'

'Why was Mr Burgan with you?'

'The day before I spoke to him on the telephone about his

conduct at work, which had been less than satisfactory ... In passing I mentioned that I was going to Southampton the following day. Kiro said he was keen to come, as he had friends he wanted to catch up with in the city. As I thought I could do with some assistance moving some furniture, which was destined for Southampton Homeless Support Services, I readily agreed.'

'Rather odd, isn't it? Inviting an employee who has been sacked on a trip.'

'I am not one to hold grudges.'

'Why did you not donate the furniture to a charity closer to home, Mr Devereux?'

'Call me Dyson, please. In answer to your question, I was killing two birds with one stone.'

'How so?'

'I was keen to attend the football match on the Saturday. Southampton versus Tottenham.'

I take the ticket stub from my wallet and pass it across the desk to her. She studies it.

'If you were planning to go to the football on Saturday, why did you go to Southampton on the Friday?'

'Because I wanted a night out. Southampton is a fun place, full of students, with a different vibe to London.'

'What time did you drop off this furniture at Southampton Homeless Support Services?'

'Three-thirty approximately. I didn't check the time. The woman and man who I met there will no doubt be able to give you the precise time I arrived. I do not have their names, but I can give you descriptions of both.'

'Was Mr Burgan with you when you dropped off this furniture?'

'No!' I sweep my hand horizontally through the air with the palm facing down. 'He was not.'

She rests her elbows on the desk and re-adopts the steepling gesture.

'You said you brought Mr Burgan along to assist with moving the furniture. Now you're saying he wasn't with you when you dropped it off.'

'Correct.'

'Where was Mr Burgan at this point?'

'Don't know. He got out of the van on the edge of Southampton and walked off.'

'Why would he do that when he wanted a lift into the city?'

'Because we had an argument.'

'What was it about?'

'I was critical of his discriminatory behaviour while employed in my department.'

'Go on.'

After outlining the issue with Rebecca that culminated in his removal, I tell her that I demand the highest standards from my employees. She says, 'Okay, so you are saying Mr Burgan did not appreciate being criticised, so he got out of the van?'

'Precisely.'

'Where did this happen?'

'Near the airport.'

'How near the airport?'

'It was on a small side road off the A335.'

'I see.' She leans back in her chair and studies me with her beady eyes. 'How come you turned off the A335 onto a small side road, if your destination was the city centre?'

'Because Mr Burgan had become rather angry. His behaviour could have compromised my driving and put the safety of other motorists in jeopardy.'

'And he just got out and walked off, did he?'

Following a nod, I raise the cup of cappuccino to my mouth and take a sip. This buys me some time. It could be a trap. They may well have received information regarding the incident in the layby. If so, it is critical to appear honest while at the same time downplaying the incident. Having lowered the cup to my thigh, I say, 'There was a minor altercation. Mr Burgan prodded and pushed me several times. I succeeded in deescalating the situation.'

Pascal crosses her arms; I polish off the cappuccino. She says, 'We have contradictory accounts of what occurred in this layby. A motorist described a man riding on another man's back, as if he were a bull at a rodeo.'

'Ludicrous!' The policeman is smirking. 'People are prone to hyperbole in these situations. If anything vaguely intriguing punctuates their banal existences, they exaggerate it, to make their lives seem more exciting.'

'Moving on. What did you do on Friday after leaving Southampton Homeless Support Services?'

After telling her about my visit to the Titanic Museum and Mexican meal, I say, 'In the evening I went to a bar in Oxford Street, Southampton's Oxford Street. They have one there too. I made the acquaintance of two female students from the university. After leaving the bar I went to their house, where I spent the night.'

'Do you remember where that was?'

'It was a house in C-C-Colton Street, I believe. Near the end of the road on the right.'

'And these girls names are?'

'Fiona and Sh-Sh-something or other.'

'Is it the case that you have so many women surrounding you all the time, you cannot remember their names?'

'Yes.'

One corner of her mouth rises. I finger the dreadlock in my pocket. She proceeds to ask me where I rented the van from. More questions ensue. I effortlessly answer them all. She terminates the interview and stands up.

'Thank you for coming in, Mr Devereux.'

'You're welcome. I hope you manage to find Kiro. Your coffee is pretty good by the way. I will be insisting the council swap their swill generator for a Nescafé vending machine like yours.'

I am reaching for the door handle when she says, 'This isn't the first missing person you've been questioned about, is it, Mr Devereux?' I swivel around. 'Frederick Lewis.'

My gold earring. I say, 'I was indeed questioned about my bipolar acquaintance's disappearance, as were numerous others.'

'You were kept in the cells overnight.'

'Indeed I was, as a result of your force's incompetence.'

'We may have some further questions for you. If you are planning to leave the area anytime soon, be sure to let us know.'

'Certainly. Good day.'

I walk out. They have nothing on me, and they know it. Darko could be anywhere. A voicemail has been left on my mobile phone. It is from Sunita. *Don't bother coming back in today. We'll see you tomorrow.* Excellent, in that case I will have some lunch and then return to my flat. The afternoon will be idled away reading *La Planète des Singes* and catching up on some sleep. It will be another late night. I have a head to collect.

*

00:13 – Having placed my copy of *La Planète des Singes* on the living room table, I take my empty wine glass through to the kitchen and put it in the dishwasher. There are numerous ways to dispose of bodies. One way is to dump non-identifiable bits in various locations, potentially over a period of time. However, with the police snooping around, it is advisable that I dispose of the body promptly. The plan is to cremate it in the new cremator. I have a key for Newton New and the cremation facility itself. I want to cremate it all at once, and to do that I need the head. The facility's overseer Simeon is currently on his annual two-week holiday in the Philippines. This suits me, as he would likely notice something was awry if a body had been

166

logged on the system that he was not aware of. Simeon is extremely vigilant when it comes to his cremators.

It is time to go to Pegasus' lair. There are no more mortuary gloves, kitchen gloves will have to suffice. I will bring my remaining tracksuit top and a bin liner to keep the head in. The handgun with the engraved stock is lying on a bookshelf in the living room. It is loaded. Carrying a gun around is reckless and not something I would usually consider. It is highly unlikely that I will require it tonight, but with so many unsavoury characters loitering in the vicinity of Hope Court, it could theoretically come in useful, if I am challenged. After all I will be in possession of a head. And if they discover I am in possession of a head, I will never hear the end of it. I only live around the corner and may well be running into said persons again. As I ruminate on whether I should bring the handgun along, I tap the toe of my trainer-clad foot on the floor. The handgun is stuffed in the waistband of my tracksuit bottoms, Pegasus-style.

Lights are on in two of the second-floor flats. The landing is deserted. Right, time to retrieve that head. I pull the tracksuit hood up, trot over to the block, bound up the stairs, and tiptoe along the landing. When I pass the two flats with their lights on, I duck, so as not to be visible to those inside. Its key is slipped into the lock and twisted. The illumination being emitted from the lava lamp is adequate, and there is no need to turn on the living room's light switch. I go through to the bedroom, close its door, and switch on the light. Having opened the wardrobe, I bend over, reach beneath the hanging street apparel, and feel about for the head. Where is it? Maybe it rolled into the corner, heads are oval shaped. It is not in this corner, or any of the corners. I part the hanging street apparel and peer down at the wardrobe's base. There is no head. The head has gone. Someone has come in here and taken it. This is far from ideal. I must leave.

The landing is unoccupied. I sneak out of the flat, gently pull the front door shut and tiptoe along the landing. From a flat comes the sound of a television, from another raised voices. After traversing the landing, I descend the stairs. I am halfway down them when I see Pegasus' accomplice advancing from the opposite direction. I bow my head and keep walking.

'Oi wasteman!' *Wasteman?* When I try and slip past him, he barges me into the railings with his shoulder. He yanks out a knife and points it at me. 'Where's his body at?' The knife edges closer to me. 'Spit it out, or I shank you straight up.'

'I have no idea what you are referring to.'

'Tell me!'

The knife is inching towards my chin. I pull the handgun from the waistband of my tracksuit bottoms and aim it at his forehead. He steps back. With the handgun aimed at him, I walk backwards down the stairs. He remains where he is. At the bottom of the stairs, I spin around. Strutting this way are three young men, two young women, and a mastiff. The accomplice shouts, 'That wasteman merked Blood Letz!'

I secrete the handgun underneath my top and take off running. The hood comes off. One of the women shrieks, 'It's da James Bond dude, innit!'

Footsteps and snarls are audible behind me. Having sprinted across the grassed area, I pull the hood up, run across a road, shoot around a corner, and dart behind a wheelie bin at the front of a high-rise apartment block.

'Where's he at?'

I crouch. A *growl* is followed by the mastiff's head appearing around the side of the bin.

'Rah, rah, rah …'

'Here, innit!'

The posse emerges from the darkness. The mastiff strains on its leash as it tries to reach me. A female member says, 'Have beef with you.'

'Know you did the one eight seven,' says the accomplice.
'Where's the body at?'

'Rah, rah, rah ...'

When I whip out the handgun, the posse backs away.

'Know where your manor's at!' Several of the members extend their arms to the left, in the direction of my block of flats. 'Watch yourself!'

'OJ us lot. We will own you.'

'This is our end, you get me?'

No, I do not, they are talking nonsense. I aim the handgun at them. They back off further. The accomplice says, 'We will merk you, mash man!'

When I step towards them, they run away.

*

08:53 – The next morning – As I pass through floor seven, I take sips from my caffè latte extra hot with soya milk. Emma is grinning at me from her desk. I say, 'Good morning.'

'*So* tired today. Casper kept me awake half the night.' *Casper? Who is Casper? Her sex mad, and presumably blind partner.* 'He was crying, running around. You name it, he was doing it. Kids eh?'

Her child, of course. As she rambles on about her son, I inspect the framed photograph of him on her desk. What an unfortunate creature. Like his mother he has an abnormally small forehead, which is completely out of proportion with the rest of the face. When she stops talking, I continue on my way. Due to the incident last night, I must leave my flat. The posse know where I live, and they are evidently extremely keen to seek revenge for their fallen leader. I will find temporary lodgings elsewhere. What with the police snooping around they will not be extravagant, as it is possible they are aware that a reward was on offer for the capture of Darko. And if they are aware of this, and see me living extravagantly, it will look suspicious. There are only three months remaining on my flat's lease.

Terrence of the failed hair transplant is trudging towards me. Scant strands of hair are clinging apologetically to his scalp.

'Morning Dyson.'

'Good morning.'

In Burials and Cemeteries, I set the cup of coffee on the desk and switch on my computer. Pegasus' posse are degenerate imbeciles. Them discovering that I am responsible for their leader's demise is iniquitous. Rakesha is tottering this way. The corners of her mouth are curled downwards. She leans over me, and says in a hushed voice, 'Why were the police with you yesterday?'

'There has been vandalism at one of my cemeteries, not for the first time.'

'Oh no!' The corners of her mouth curl upwards. 'That's terrible. Um, do you want to do something after work today? I have a bit of spare time before I collect my daughter. A drink maybe?'

'Sure, let's do that.'

Having looked left and right, she kisses me on the cheek and rubs the inside of my thigh. She totters off. During the drink, I will inform Rakesha that I am only prepared to continue seeing her on a casual basis. After the drink, I will look for suitable accommodation, and then cremate the body. It is still in the Mini Metro. I recline in the revolving office chair and look up at the ceiling. While the posse are no doubt dangerous, the good news is they will not be informing the authorities of their suspicion that I was responsible for their leader's demise. It is not street culture to talk to the police.

I am returning from the printer with some printouts when I see that my guzzling subordinate has arrived. It is smirking.

'Sunita just phoned. She said you have to go up to her office, right away.'

I put on my suit jacket and make my way through the office to the stairs. Sunita will attempt to delve for more information about what occurred with the police. Its prying will be in vain. Darren is jogging down the stairs. He is wearing office trousers and black Nike trainers.

'Alright!'

'Good morning.'

'Police snoopin' about you is what I heard. Big shit you're in, I reckon.' He stops. 'Frank wouldn't let on much but can tell it's a biggie. Well fill me in, you cunt?'

'I'm busy.'

'You're a dark horse you are, Dyson.'

Sunita is sitting at its desk. The head of finance is standing beside it. I knock on the glass door. She says, 'Enter.'

When I walk in, the head of finance crosses his spindly arms. He is doing a good impression of an anorexic bouncer. I say, 'Good morning. How can I be of assistance?'

Sunita spits, 'Sit down!'

I lower myself onto a chair. It glares at me from the other side of the desk. *Bindi explode, bindi explode, bindi explode.* Following a slurp of cappuccino, it says, 'The police poling up was a surprise and a major embarrassment.' It places henna-stained appendages on the desk. 'It was the first time in all my years here that the police have showed up wanting to question one of our staff.' It twists its head to the side. 'How about you Ishmael? Have the police ever come to question anyone while you've worked here?'

He says 'No' through the corner of his mouth.

'Your dealings with this Kiro chap have been ruinous for your career here.' It leans across the desk. 'What we don't understand is how you would allow that homophobic brute to destroy your career.' *Because of the Euros.* 'I would wipe that smile off your face if I was you.' *You are not me; you are nothing compared to me.* 'Firstly, you were in serious breach of

171

our regulations by not reporting the homophobic abuse directed at one of our own. Then the police show up. From what they were saying, it seems you had dealings with that man after he was fired from here. This is unbelievably poor judgement. Don't you agree, Ishmael?'

'Yes,' he says through the corner of his mouth.

'Well, what's been going on?' A henna-smeared finger protrudes in my direction. 'Explain yourself?'

'Stop pointing at me and I will tell you.' It tuts and lowers its finger. 'Kiro has purportedly disappeared, as you are aware. The police seemed to think I was one of the last people to see him.'

'I know. And why would they think that?'

'Because I ran into him on the high street the week after his contract was terminated.'

Sunita scrawls on a notepad. It looks up at me, and says, 'What happened, exactly?'

'Nothing. He grunted at me, I said hello. That was it.'

'Find that hard to believe.' The red smear that serves as its mouth smirks. 'We're expected to believe that's all that happened.' It leans across the desk again. 'Might I remind you that I am one of the most senior employees here at the council. You answer to me. I suggest you start talking, if you want to salvage what is left of your career here.' It folds its arms. 'Well, I will try another question then. What happened at the police station? Go on!'

'At the police station I had a cappuccino from their Nescafé vending machine. It serves coffee that is vastly superior to the swill dispensed by the machine on this floor, that you so readily guzzle, *Sunita*.' Its eyebrows raise. 'I suggest Ishmael, as you are finance's supremo, that you invest in a Nescafé machine.'

He looks down at the floor. It murmurs, 'You are obviously a sick man.'

'Quite the contrary, I am exceedingly healthy. If there is nothing else, I will be on my way.'

'Yes, you certainly will be. You are hereby suspended. While this matter is under investigation you will remain on full pay. I wouldn't hold your breath if I were you. The chances of you returning here are pretty slim.' I stifle a yawn with the back of my hand. 'What we need from you now are the keys to the cemeteries and other facilities. Where are they?'

'Left hand drawer in my desk.'

It picks up a telephone handset, and says into it, 'Sunita here. Go to Dyson's desk and get the keys from ...' *I have copies of all the keys, including for the crematorium where I will be heading later, and Newton Old where my stash of Euros is awaiting.* 'You're still smiling? Why is that?'

Because I am swamped with Euros and have added a new memento to my collection. Sunita and Ishmael watch me in silence. Seven years at the forefront of the death industry has come to an end. *Veni, vidi, vici.* I came, I saw, I conquered. Newton Borough's Burials and Cemeteries department survived world wars and a plague, but it has faced nothing as calamitous as my impending departure. The damage will be severe and permanent. On the desk a telephone is ringing. It picks it up, and says into it, 'Thank you.' It sets it down. 'Dyson, do you have all your personal effects?'

'Yes.'

'We will escort you from the building. Stand up.'

On the journey through floor eight, I pass Frank. He glances at me and shakes his head, the motion small but rapid. Ishmael and it follow me into the lift. The lift descends to the ground floor. I disembark, as do they. Next to the lifts there is an umbrella stand. I pluck an umbrella from it.

'Put that back!' spits Sunita. 'It's not yours.'

I hold the handle to my shoulder, aim the tip of the umbrella at the *bindi* in the middle of its head, and squeeze my right index finger.

'BOOM!'

Sunita squeals and dives into a lift.

FOURTEEN

1 9:08 – THAT EVENING – I am on the sofa in my living room reading *Le Pont de la Rivière Kwai*. I have finished *Planète des Singes*. Prior to commencing reading, I searched on the internet for some suitable accommodation. A cheap hotel called The Newton Inn is my current preference. They have vacancies. Eva gets out of rehab the day after tomorrow and she will require an explanation as to why I am not staying in my flat. Having rested the book on my chest, I ponder what I will tell her. The best course of action is to simply say that the posse have been demanding additional payments and that I am refusing to pay, hence my decision to vacate my residence for the time being in case they seek retaliation. Will they start harassing her too, in an attempt to find out where I am? Perhaps the best course of action is that we go away for a while. Maybe the continent, possibly France or Italy, or both. However not quite yet, as the police may have plans to waste more of their time in questioning me further.

I have just resumed reading when there is a loud *bang* on the front door. Who is that? I am not expecting anyone. Could the posse have gained access to my building? While they seemingly somehow know I live in here, they presumably don't know which flat I reside in. *Bang! Bang!* I put the book on the coffee table, tiptoe over to the door, and peer through the peephole. An elderly man is shuffling from side to side. It is Eva's neighbour, the man who lent me the car. I remove the door chain, open the door, and say, 'Good evening.'

'It's me.'

'So I see.'

'Knew you lived in here somewhere. One of your neighbours told me which flat. Want my car back, this minute. Got dinner at my sister's in ...' He looks at his wrist. 'An hour. Was under the impression you only needed it for a bit and would be returning it pronto. Well give me the key and I'll be out of your hair.'

'Your car is currently unavailable.'

'What does that mean?'

'I can bring it to you first thing tomorrow. It is presently elsewhere.'

'No, it's not. Saw it parked round the back of here.'

'It cannot be returned today.'

He throws an arm up, and says, 'Give me the key!'

'No.'

'You'd think it was you doing me the favour. Where's Eva? She won't be impressed by this. I want a word with her. Only lent it to you in the first place because you said it was to help her out. Or is she currently unavailable as well? She weren't at home.'

'She is indeed unavailable.'

'Jesus Christ!'

'This is what I can do for you.'

'Go on.'

'Pay for you to be ferried to and fro from your sister's in a taxi.'

'Why not give me my car back and save yourself the money.'

'Because I have a delivery to do in your car.'

'Whatever! Twenty quid each way then.' He clicks his fingers. 'Cough it up.' I give him two twenty-pound notes from my wallet. 'First thing tomorrow. And I trust no shady business is going on with my motor. This all sounds pretty fishy to me.'

*

00:16 – Having pulled up at the gates to Newton New, I wait in the Mini Metro while two inebriated youths stumble past. When they have disappeared, I disembark, unlock the gate, get in the Mini Metro, drive into the cemetery, alight, lock the gate, get in the Mini Metro, and with the lights turned off drive slowly along the path that bisects the burial ground. The entrance to Newton New is of course monitored by CCTV. However, if there is no suspicion that an incident has occurred here, no one will be checking the footage. And there will be no suspicion, as I am a consummate professional. Besides, the number plates have been covered up and I am unrecognisable in a hat and non-descript coat. The outlines of headstones are visible in the darkness. On my left, I can make out the contours of a cherub. Essex Cherubs are considerably less offensive when viewed at night.

The car is parked behind the chapel. I disembark and do a circuit of the funeral hall, looking through windows as I go. All the lights inside are off, as they should be. Somewhere in the cemetery an owl is *hooting*. Owls are rarely heard or seen in London, even here in the suburbs. When I approach the entrance, the security light switches on. I unlock the door, go inside, and walk through to the cremator room. Where is the corpse trolley? There it is. I wheel it out to the Mini Metro, load it with the wrapped body parts, and then push it through to the cremator room.

I am perched on Simeon's office chair, surveying the cremator's control panel. For such a simple steel structure, the CT III is rather complex. There are two rows of lights, each with six buttons. What are these down here? Connecting MS pipelines,

176

fresh air blower, scrubber with cyclone separator, ID fan, digital meters. Time to get the Kanthal electric heating furnace on ... Log in to the computer with the password, Ashes2Ashes69 ... The body's details need to be inputted. For the name, I opt for Ignōtus, and for the required four-digit alphanumerical code, B314. The dead drug addict who was cremated here was designated B313.

In an ideal world, I would delete the details when I'm done, leaving no record of a cremation having taken place here. However, this does not appear to be possible. Well, no one will put two and two together. It is fortunate that Simeon is on holiday. Two temporary cremation managers are conducting cremations at a reduced rate in his absence. They will assume the other conducted this cremation. The cremator's hatch spring opens. I shove the trolley over to it and slide the plastic-wrapped body inside. Incinerating plastic is not eco-friendly, but this is a one off. Next up is the legs. And now for the arms.

'Don't be shy; get in there.' When the hatch is closed, the body parts are instantly engulfed in flames. I take a seat on the chair, interlock my fingers behind my neck and watch it burn through the window in the hatch. 'You should be grateful that despite your insufferable behaviour, I am not sending you from this world to the accompaniment of Celine Dion's wails.'

*

Two hours later – Newton Old – The tools and materials that were employed for the killing and ensuing dismembering have been soaked in bleach. I am presently shoving them in a hole, which I have just dug. Its mobile is dropped in too. Having covered it with earth and a sprinkling of leaves, I amble over to the tomb where my stash is being stored. I lower my arm into it, hook the clothes hanger attached to my belt to the top of the bag, and hoist it up. A wad of Euros is removed from the bag.

From a coat pocket, I extract the fly-fishing tin my mother bought me for my seventh birthday. I hold the torch in my mouth and caress the contents – crucifix necklace, earring, monocle, dreadlock, pigtail. When I touch nemesis Beatrice's pigtail, I see my fourteen-year-old self peering down at it. *Pull me up! Pull me up I said!* When I take the penknife from my pocket, it stops pleading and starts wailing. I bend over and saw off one of its braided pigtails. *NO!* I swipe its fingers off the cliff edge with my foot. *Help!* It plummets shrieking into the mist.

I am stroking the latest addition to my collection. In the torch light, the yellow, green and red cotton threads seem to sliver, as if they were snakes. I am kneeling astride of it. As the syringe descends, it stares up at me and squirms frantically. There is a *squelch* as the needle passes through the pupil. Its body convulses violently. The spasms become feebler; the body goes slack.

My fly-fishing tin is placed in the bag containing the Euros. The bag is lowered into the tomb. What with the posse hassling me, the police investigating me, and as I am poised to move to temporary lodgings, it is for the best that my most treasured possessions remain hidden away for the time being. I will return for them soon.

FIFTEEN

THE FOLLOWING DAY – The Newton Inn – My room here is furnished with a single bed, a chair, a plywood wardrobe, and an out-dated television that displays nothing but static unless banged repeatedly with a fist. The bathroom has the same dimensions as an aeroplane toilet. It is windowless, bereft of ventilation, and has a shower that spits water as if it were obscenities. As for the Newton Inn's guests, many are refugee looking types, no doubt housed here by the council. There are women in brightly coloured dresses and dishevelled children clasping harmonicas. It is only a matter of time before a dancing bear makes an appearance.

There are solitary men too. I have seen them loitering furtively outside rooms clutching dreary bouquets of flowers, glancing at wristwatches, and wiping sweat from their furrowed foreheads. On two occasions today, I have witnessed scantily clad women immersed in cheap perfume usher men into rooms. This hotel-cum-asylum centre must make a small fortune from its room-by-the-hour service.

Earlier, I went to the basement to take a look at the facilities. There is a launderette down there. A searingly hot room, whose only source of illumination is provided by a flickering length of ceiling lighting. There was a young woman in the launderette stuffing sheets into a drying machine. We conversed. This evening I am taking the convivial gum chewing Albanian out for dinner.

I am presently in the foyer, perched on a moth-eaten armchair beside a plastic palm tree, flicking through a week-old copy of the *Newton Post*. What a worthless rag it is. I place it on the rim of the plastic palm tree's pot. Mother didn't do much for me during her prematurely terminated existence, but in her defence, she did gift me my fly-fishing tin. And she had the prescience to get a large one. There is still room for a couple more mementos in it. I wonder what they will be. My dinner date is running late. I peer up at the ceiling and ponder my soon-to-be improved life. It won't be long until I am on the continent. There I will do as I please all day every day. My time at the council will be a distant memory. She has just alighted from the lift. Her black hair is styled in a bouffant and she is wearing a sparkling mini dress. Think Diana Ross meets Eastern Bloc.

'Hiya!'

I stand up, and say, 'Good evening.'

'Where are we going?'

'Ristorante Toscana.'

'Italian, yes?'

'Correct.'

'Love Italian food.'

It is the same restaurant I went to with Rakesha.

*

Eighteen hours later – I am approaching Earls Court tube station, where I am due to meet Eva. It is a sunny day and there are a lot of people milling around on the street. My mobile phone is vibrating. I pluck it from my trouser pocket and inspect the screen. Whose number is this?

'Good afternoon. Who is this?'

'It's me!' *Ah, Rakesha. Who gave her my number? Must have been Frank. No one else had it there.* 'Dyson, are you there?'

'Yes.'

'What is going on? People in the office are saying you've been suspended or even sacked. Is this true?'

'No, it is not.'

'Okay, so what the hell's going on then? Does this have anything to do with the police I saw you with? You said it was just something to do with your cemeteries. But seems a bit odd the police showed up at the office and the next moment you're gone.' I stop walking. 'Talk to me!'

'My absence has nothing to do with the police.'

'So, what has it got to do with then ...? Come on, I deserve an explanation. If you haven't been suspended or sacked, what is it? Dyson!'

'You're cutting out.' I hold the device away from my ear. 'Can't hear you.'

'Hello, can you hear me?'

I hang up, block her number, and continue walking. Eva emerges from the tube station. She emits a loud shriek as she races towards me. The colour has returned to her youthful cheeks, and she is her vivacious, graceful, pre-drug dependent self once more. Having leapt through the air, she throws her arms around my neck and kisses me forcefully on the mouth.

'It's amazing to see you! I missed you.' She holds my hand. We walk along the pavement. 'I'm so grateful you paid for me to go to rehab. It was great. Was a bit stressful at first, but soon got into the swing of things. I feel good and ready to move on with my life. And so looking forward to Christmas.' She squeezes my hand. 'Anyway, how have you been?'

'Fine. Everything has been going well.'

'Any news?'

'No, nothing to report. It's been uneventful.'

'Work okay?'

'Yes, work is good.'

'Cool. Let me tell you all about rehab then. Everything was really structured, like every single day. Which sounds kind of boring, yet it wasn't. We'd wake up at six and … What's the plan?'

'We are having lunch at a Chinese around the corner.'

'Fabulous, love Chinese. Where was I? Oh yeah, after breakfast we had morning reflection and meditation, then exercise and group behavioural therapy …' *I am thinking vegetable spring rolls and a prawn dish. This high-end establishment will not be serving reconstituted crab claws. One of London's most famous cemeteries is down that road on the right.* Eva pulls on my arm. 'What are you looking over there for?'

'There is a well-known necropolis down there.'

'Necropolis?'

'A burial ground.'

She slaps my shoulder, and says, '*Please* no burial grounds, cemeteries, whatever.' We are a few metres from the restaurant when she swivels to face me. 'In a perfect world I would take a break from here for a while. Get away from everything. Do something new.' She squeezes my hand again. 'But not without you of course, so guess it will have to wait. You've got your work after all.'

'I was actually thinking of going to Europe for an extended break.'

'What about your job?'

'As I have transformed my department into the council's most successful and efficiently run division, I am to be rewarded with a sabbatical.'

'Fantastic! And you said you didn't have any news. When did you find out about this? You never told me anything about it.'

'It has been in the pipeline for a while, but has only just been finalised. I wanted it to be a surprise.'

'It's a surprise alright. Wonderful news that is. We can go away together, soon I hope. It'll be great.'

Eva's enthusiasm may be dampened somewhat when she hears that I have vacated my flat and am residing in a budget hotel.

Dyson is only just getting started. Follow his further adventures in #2 Sepultura.

Please leave a review for Necropolis. Reviews are vital to us authors for finding new readers.

Printed in Great Britain
by Amazon

11054228R00109